"Aliens!" Cletus stopped in balance and joined Bubbah o stared. The front door of tl bartenders glanced out. He still held a towel in his hand, and he didn't look happy.

Cletus glanced at him, then back at the guy on the ground.

"Calm down, Bubbah," he said, and tell me what you saw.

"My name ain't Bubbah," the guy spit. His lip was still quivering, but as Cletus came fully into carbon-based alcohol fueled life-form focus, he looked a little less crazed. He stared up at Cletus, blinked, and went on.

"My name ain't Bubbah," he repeated, "and you ain't an alien."

"Two for two," Cletus replied. "You want to tell me what the blue Jesus you're talking about?"

"Name's Earl," the guys said. "Earl Suggs."

"Nice to meet you, Earl," Cletus replied. He caught movement out of the corner of his eye and knew that either the bartender, or someone else from the bar, was approaching quickly. "You want to tell me what you were screaming about? And while you're at it, why would you think I was an alien?"

"Abduction," Earl said, as if he hadn't heard Cletus at all. "It was a goddamned abduction, right here at the Gin."

Cletus thought fast. He had about thirty seconds before half the drunken population of The Cotton Gin closed in on the two of them, and after that he probably wouldn't get coherent word out of Earl here.

Copyright © 2017 by David Niall WIson
Cover by Zach McCain
ISBN 978-1-946025-81-4
All rights reserved. No part of this book may be used or reproduced in any manner whatsoever without written permission except in the case of brief quotations embodied in critical articles and reviews.
For information address Crossroad Press at 141 Brayden Dr., Hertford, NC 27944
A Macabre Ink Production - Macabre Ink is an imprint of Crossroad Press.
www.crossroadpress.com

First Trade Edition

The Not Quite Right Reverend Cletus J. Diggs

&

The Currently Accepted Habits of Nature

by DAVID NIALL WILSON

Everything Connects

By David Niall Wilson

Sometimes stories travel their own roads, taking off in a straight line, or curving in and out of plots, on the way to their tidy ending. This book that you hold in your hands does that – it has a plot, it has a beginning, body, and conclusion. It stands alone, but in this case, that's not where it ends. I don't' know how it is for other authors. I don't pretend to know the right way a thing should be done; I only know the way that seems right to me.

My characters and settings are drawn from the world of my experience. Sometimes I have a hard time digging up the original references that spawn them, but I always do if I give it enough thought, because possibly the most impossible task in writing, to my mind, would be to make up a story and a populate it with characters where nothing that I've seen or experienced could influence the plot, populated by characters with no characteristics similar to anyone I've ever met, seen on a television show, or read about in another book. In other words, the worlds of my stories are built from pieces salvaged from my life.

Some of the settings and characters resonate more fully than others. I guess everything in life is that way. We like certain foods better than others, root for sports teams, paint things different colors, or don't paint them at all. When you find what matters to you, you keep it and you care for it, and that's what I've done throughout my career as an author. I have a collection of places and faces that I enjoy revisiting, and more often than not, they end up blurring and blending.

Cletus J. Diggs is a jack-of-all-trades in a serious sense. He is a journalist, an investigator, an ordained minister, a practicing common-law lawyer, and many other things I've not yet discovered, but that I have no doubt exist. This is the novel where I first introduced him: The Not Quite Right Reverend Cletus J. Diggs & the Currently Accepted Habits of Nature. The title comes from a quote by physicist Richard Feynman, who commented that as often as they change, we really have no "laws of nature," but only "the currently accepted habits". That stuck with me.

One day I went running, and I saw a big banner stretched across the main street of the town where we lived at the time – Hertford, NC – announcing the upcoming Harvest Festival. I've read a lot about the origins of such festivals. I've also read books like Harvest Home by Thomas Tryon. I know that a lot of things came to America from the old world and put down new roots.

Anyone who has been near something as amazing as The Great Dismal Swamp, knows that – if there are old powers alive and well in or on this planet, they will gather, and be more powerful, in older places. There are lines of energy crisscrossing the planet – Ley Lines, some call them. Old Mill is a junction – a place where those lines cross – a place where there is greater potential for strange things to happen – probably a magnet for them.

In this first novel, Cletus gets caught up in swamp magic, genetic experimentation, swamp witches and a whole lot of redneckery. With his buddy Jasper, Sheriff Bob, and several others tagging along and getting in the way, he encounter everything from alien visitation to albino twins, and the Great Horned God of the old Religion.

That was a fun novel to write. It has been very popular, both in print, and in audio – and remains available in eBook and Audiobook formats. At that point I sort of left Cletus behind, and moved on to other projects.

The longest running series that I have is The DeChance Chronicles, starting with Heart of a Dragon, set in my fictional city of San Valencez (born of memories I collected living in San Diego, California). This is followed by Vintage Soul, which was actually written and published first, but ended up number two, chronologically. I know, it's confusing. Trust me, read Heart of a Dragon first.

San Valencez is one of my other go-to settings. A lot of my novels have taken place there, and over the years, the walls between stories have softened, and often broken. In Book III of The DeChance Chronicles, My Soul to Keep, which is a novella, I tell the origin story of Donovan DeChance, how he got his powers, and started on the long, long life that led into the present day. The town where this novel was set – Rookwood – is also the setting of the novel Hallowed Ground, which I wrote with author Steven Savile. Many of the characters from that story – or at least, their ancestors – appear in My Soul to Keep. I love that town, and that world. I'm sure I'll go back to it.

Then came Book IV of The DeChance Chronicles, Kali's Tale. This book tells the story of the vampire Kali, who sets out on a "blood quest" to kill the creature that created her. As it turns out – that ancient vampire lived near Old Mill, North Carolina, in – you probably already guessed – The Great Dismal Swamp. Many of the characters from the first Cletus J. Diggs novel, including Cletus himself, make appearances. Nettie – the swamp witch / earth mother plays a major part. Any time things get too close to the swamp, she seems to be involved.

There are also cameo appearances by Geoffrey Bullfinch and Rebecca York, core characters in the original series O.C.L.T., created with Aaron Rosenberg. Donovan isn't much of a 'joiner,' bug on occasion his path, and that of O.C.L.T. – a government agency created to deal with the paranormal and unexplained – cross paths. They will cross over more fully in book V.

Then I wrote the novel Nevermore, a Novel of Love, Loss & Edgar Allan Poe. This novel was meant to be a flashback at the beginning of the next DeChance novel. It grew into a story that needed a lot of space, so I cut it free and wrote it as a stand-alone novel. Of course, it takes place in The Great Dismal Swamp. Nettie is there. At one point – Donovan has a cameo. All of the stories harmonize in strange, very satisfying ways. At least, they are satisfying to me, and I have had no complaints.

Still, the whole situation begged this introduction. I spend a lot of time explaining to people why – even though Nevermore is a stand-alone work – it's better to have read this first Cletus J. Diggs novel and at least Kali's Tale before starting it. Not because you need them to love the story – but because the make it more complete. Because it's all one, big story if you read it that way.

And of course – that was not the end, either. The next novel in the DeChance Chronicles, A Midnight Dreary, brings back Donovan, the agents of the O.C.L.T., Cletus, and most of the characters from Nevermore, including Edgar Allan Poe and Lenore – and will also revisit the setting and story of my novel Darkness Falling, which I believed would be a stand-alone vampire novel.

I hope that you'll enjoy these worlds I have created, and I hope that you'll forgive me when the walls between stories thin and turn to smoke. It's how I work. If you are truly interested in my writing, it would be a good idea to read some of the earlier books – Deep Blue, Ancient Eyes, This is My Blood, Darkness Falling (This one directly impacts Nevermore and the upcoming Book V of the DeChance Chronicles). The Cletus books go without saying – you have the second one on your reader, in your hand, or on your MP3 player, or these words would never have reached you. There is also a single stand-alone Cletus Mystery – The Not Quite Right Reverend Cletus J. Diggs & the Fruit of Another Vine – which appears at the end of the eBook edition of the first Cletus book. That one was inspired by an actual vine that grows – every year – in the shape of a woman, pointing a gun into the woods behind a particular house on highway 17. The house exists…the rest you can believe, or just enjoy.

I also write short stories, and poetry. There are a number of my short story collections out there. Defining Moments was nominated for the Bram Stoker Award, and the story "The Gentle Brush of Wings," which appears in that collection, won the short fiction award that same year. If you like short stories, you might give a glance at "The Whirling Man & Others, The Call of Distant Shores, The Fall of the House of Escher & Other Illusions, and others. Some of the stories in those collections were the skeletal beginnings of novels. Deep Blue started as a novella, as did This is My Blood. If you were to make your way through all the stories and novels, you'd find a lot of those stories taking place in San Valencez California, Random Illinois, and Old Mill, North Carolina. I think, by now, you see what I'm getting at.

I have a lot of tattoos. People have asked me over the years how many I have. I always answer – one. It just has a lot of open space in it so far. It's the same with the novels and stories. The odds are, when it's all said and done, I'll find they are just one story – one that I haven't completed yet. If that's true, we'd better get on with it.

Welcome to Old Mill, NC. Enjoy your stay.

At the end of this novel, you will find a stand-alone Cletus J. Diggs short story, and previews of both The Crazy Case of Foreman James, and Crockatiel – novels also featuring Cletus J. Diggs.

CONTENTS

The Currently Accepted Habits of Nature	1
Bonus Story – The Fruit of Another Vine	97
Novel Preview – The Crazy Case of Foreman James	111
Preview – Crockatiel – A Novel of the O.C.L.T.	129

CHAPTER ONE

Near the Great Dismal Swamp, everything grows. Bugs thrive. Plants barely hesitate between frost and full, pollen-bearing bloom. A warm winter week can produce things that should sleep until summer. It's in the earth. Birth, rebirth – death.

Whatever grows must decompose. That is truth. As the sun set in a splash of deep violet and dark purple above the tree line, Jasper Winslow was contemplating that truth.

Some things decompose faster than others. Some things return to the food chain a few rungs lower than where they began. Boot leather, Jasper noted, was a durn site more resilient than denim, and a whole hell of a lot tougher than hide. Hair and teeth stood the test of time better than eyeballs or tongues, and were a lot less tantalizing to the aforementioned food chain, though bone seemed to have made it into a lower rung, at the least.

"Christ," Jasper observed eloquently. When he spoke that thought it came out more like "Keee Reist," but the meaning was clear. He was wishing some power greater than he were available to sort things out.

Reaching into his breast pocket, Jasper drew forth a battered pack of Zig Zag rolling papers and his tobacco. It was time for some serious thinking, and Jasper didn't reckon he should do that on an empty lung. Empty head was one thing; lungs needed smoke to survive – so his ol' Pap'd said. Jasper's fingers trembled, but he managed to roll a passable smoke and lit it with a match from the Red Apple convenience store out on 17.

Jasper had only been hoping for a good day fishing. The catfish were fat and hungry, and so was Jasper. It had seemed the perfect way to spend the day, despite the fact he was supposed to be fixing the air conditioning unit down at the Weller place. Air would still be there when he was done, near as he figured, and they could condition it as well tomorrow as today, though he knew he'd get an earful when he finally showed up. Things always got done in their time.

Glancing down at the edge of the swamp, where two size twelve (if they were an inch) Redwing work boots poked out of the weeds and trailed back toward the water and what remained of a man, Jasper sighed. No fish today, he knew. No air conditionin' neither. Nothin' to do but to think, just for a while, then decide what to do. One thing he knew for sure, he couldn't let this guy rot so close to his favorite fishing hole. Folks would find it, for one thing, and for another, who knew what rotted flesh would do to the water? It was a swamp, sure, but did that mean you had to by-God pollute it?

The cigarette he'd rolled burned low, flame slipping up one side cantankerously, and Jasper hurriedly licked the side that was burning so the other could catch up. He didn't want to waste the tobacco – it wasn't cheap.

He leaned in closer, letting the ash drop from his smoke onto the soaked denim of the man's jeans. There wasn't much to see from where he stood. The water sucked at the waist of the man's pants, and everything above the chest was obscured by plants and mud. Jasper didn't really want to know what was going on with the parts beneath that murky surface, but it didn't seem right to leave the man in the swamp.

He reached down, ready to grip those boots and yank the body free of the mud, and he stopped. It wasn't that he was squeamish, but what he'd just noticed sat him back on his heels. Jasper wasn't the sharpest tool in the shed, so his ol' Pap had said, but he had a good eye for things. What caught that eye just then were branches. Where the man's head should have been, there was the oddest set of branches jutting from the water that Jasper had ever seen. They weren't really like branches at all, in fact, but he couldn't quite put his finger on why they weren't like branches. They had the requisite slime and moss, and they were muddy as hell.

"Probably roots," he muttered to himself, not believing it for a second. The itch in the back of his mind was stronger, and he'd lost all interest in grabbing those boots. Another thought had imbedded itself in his mind, and he backed away with a quick grunt. Jasper watched a lot of TV. Not that reality Tee Vee, or any of that science fiction crap, but the real stuff. Cops, killers, guns and drama. He watched WWE Smackdown, when it was on, but Jasper had other thoughts on his mind just that moment. This was a by-God crime scene. Unless the man he was about to grab had tripped face first in the swamp, turned on his back, and drowned one hell of a clumsy death, someone had dropped him here. There might be prints. There might be evidence. Hell, he'd probably trampled over half of it already, and wouldn't it be a wonderful thing to add his fingerprints to the mix? Then, there were those roots, or branches, or whatever the hell they were to think about.

Jasper looked down at the silent, motionless form, half-covered in swamp mud and slime, and shook his head.

"Huh uh," he grunted. "Ain't draggin' ol' Jasper into this one. No way."

Turning, he headed back toward his truck, wanting to break into a run and controlling the urge in a sort of half-stumble, half speed-walk that would have looked to even the most casual observer like a man on the lam from the Devil. Jasper had that level of cool. Of course, there was no one within a mile to see him, so the performance went unnoticed. He reached his beat up Ford pickup, climbed in, and fired the engine, even as he reached for a cold Milwaukee's Best from the cooler on the passenger side floorboard. With practiced ease, he snapped the top and poured half the can down his throat.

Hell of a thing, he thought. Man finds a dead guy in the swamp and has to sneak a beer just to keep from being caught with it on the highway.

Briefly, Jasper thought about going to the police. Then, with uncharacteristic wisdom, he glanced at the half-empty beer can in his hand, and thought again. There was only one place to go with this. There was only one man who might understand, or, barring that, take the matter off Jasper's hands and let him get on with his fishing.

Jasper slugged the second half of his beer, tossed the can out the window, and slammed the truck into drive. It was only about five miles to Cletus Diggs' trailer, and there were back roads all the way. That was another plus. With a grin, Jasper reached out and grabbed a second beer.

Jasper turned down a winding, rutted lane that curled around a stand of trees just off 17. If you were on the highway, you'd never suspect the place existed. Cletus Diggs was a private man, most times, and he liked folks to respect that.

There was a mailbox standing beside that outer road. Beneath the battered tin box, a string of small signs unfolded, like the credit cards from a city man's wallet. The Reverend Cletus J. Diggs. Cletus J. Diggs – Attorney at Law. Diggs Investigations – nothing buried so deep we can't dig it out. There were more. Nearly a dozen, by Jasper's closest guess. Cletus wasn't a man to let any dollar lie outside the circle of his influence. Jasper ignored the signs and turned into the long drive that led back to Cletus' trailer. To Jasper, Cletus was just Cletus, no more, no less, and no amount of mail-order schooling or chest-puffing would change that. Jasper and Cletus had grown up together, fished the swamp and hunted the hills since both had been short enough to arm wrestle a snake.

Cletus' Bronco was parked out front, and the old air conditioning unit was pumping its heart out. This was another reason Jasper wasn't impressed with Cletus. For all his prancing about and big words, it was Jasper who'd had to fix the air conditioning, re-pipe the plumbing and wire up the satellite dish jutting out at an odd angle from the trailer's roof. Among the signs dangling from the mailbox of Mr. Cletus J. Diggs, there were none that required an ability to work with his hands.

Jasper pulled in beside the Bronco and killed his engine. He grabbed what remained of the twelve-pack and crawled out of the truck. There was a doorbell on the trailer, but Jasper ignored it. Half the time Cletus ignored it himself and this was too important to get into a tussle over. This was big-time, Jasper told himself – the real deal. The man that never had a thing happen in his life had run smack into a wall of something and it was going to be up to Cletus to sort it out. That is, assuming Cletus wanted that AC pump to keep blowin' cold air all summer and his toilet to flush.

The trailer was dimly lit, half the illumination coming from a shuttered window across from the door, and the rest from a lamp at the far end. That lamp sat on an old wooden desk, canted to one side and held up by three legs and a stack of old law books.

Cletus kept the law books around "for show," and though Jasper and several clients had pointed out that the law books were from Kentucky, and over 100 years old, Cletus just smiled and nodded, being Cletus. "It's not like I'm going to read the damn things," he'd say. "They just help with the ambiance of the office."

Office. Jasper had nearly snorted beer through his nose. The corner of that trailer was about as much a law office as his pickup truck was a NASCAR champion. There were papers scattered over every available surface and sifting into cracks in search of new ones. There were cups and cans, pizza boxes and cigar packs lying about in such profusion you'd have thought the trailer was a recycling bin for old paper products.

In the middle of it all, on the far side of the desk, Cletus Jehosephat Diggs looked up from where he'd been hard at work on the Weekly World News crossword puzzle, startled.

"There's an amazing new product," Cletus said, regaining his composure. "No bigger than a baseball. They attach it to the outside of your house, and those folks with more manners than a swamp rat push the button in the center. It announces their arrival."

Jasper ignored Cletus and slapped a beer on top of the pile of papers on the near side of his friend's desk. "This here swamp rat-mannered, no-account, don't give a fuck in hell about your announcement-buttoned doohickey redneck is gonna put you in a world of hurt if you don't pop the top on that beer and listen up."

Cletus frowned, but the expression didn't hold. Grinning, he grabbed the offered beer and leaned back.

"I take it this isn't purely a social call," he said, grin widening.

"It is not," Jasper agreed, taking a long slug from his beer. "I'm in a bit of a fix, Cletus. I thought you might offer some professional advice."

"Get another of those Edenton girls pregnant?" Cletus asked, arching one eyebrow and watching his friend with interest. "Hit someone's livestock with your truck? You haven't been tippin' cows without me, have you Jaz?"

Jasper grunted. "Stop it, Cletus," he said. "I'm serious this time. I ran into something today – somethin' I'm not sure what to do with."

Cletus sat up again. Jasper was never serious. Never. There

had been a tornado sweeping through the county a few months back, houses with the roofs sucked clean off and garages spinning on their foundations, and Jasper's idea of a good way to spend that historic moment had been to drive into the storm and see if he could hit the center. Luckily for Jasper, and every building and living being within range of the pickup, the storm had lifted off and left him with nothing but a rain of golf-ball-sized hail for his trouble. The insurance had refused, at first, to pay, and it was only Cletus' timely intervention on his friend's behalf that had gotten the damage repaired, and the claims adjustor out of an early retirement, courtesy of an irate Jasper.

"Okay, Jaz," Cletus said soberly, sipping his beer to belie the fact. "Tell me what's on your mind."

It didn't take Jasper long to fill Cletus in on the facts, as he knew them. This was mostly due to the fact that Jasper didn't really know a damn thing, except that there was a dead man sticking boots first out of the swamp, and that someone (not Jasper) needed to fetch the police and drag that guy out. That, and that there was a clump of roots poking long, slender fingers out of the swamp that was going to visit his dreams for a long time to come. He didn't mention that part. Cletus would see for himself, or he wouldn't see a damn thing. Jasper could wait to see which it was. He could wait a long damn time.

"You didn't touch him?" Cletus asked, not really a question. Jasper had the familiar sense that the gears in Cletus' surprisingly agile mind had engaged fully. The crossword was pushed aside and forgotten, the spreading ring of condensation from Cletus' beer defacing a photograph of two enormously fat people in shorts they should never have owned, standing on the cracked surface of a tennis court.

"TOO-FAT TWINS WRECK TENNIS CAMP – OWNER SERVES THEM WITH COURT" was emblazoned in bold letters across the top of the now sodden page.

Cletus was paying no attention to Jasper, or the Weekly World News. If the fat twins weren't looking for a lawyer, Cletus wasn't interested, and to explain the legalities of damage suits to Jasper would take more years and beers than either of them had left. Cletus was thinking. There were a lot of angles you could take on a dead man in the swamp, particularly if you were a man of as many talents and professions as Cletus Diggs.

Finally, gulping the last of his beer and sending the can in a failed arc toward the can in the corner, already buried in a pile of prior bad shots, he pushed back his chair and stood.

"You did the right thing, Jasper. I'll handle it."

Jasper nodded, still frowning at the fat twins in the article. "What you going to do, Cletus?"

"Not sure yet," Cletus replied. "First I'm going to go have me a look. Then I'm going to call the police and meet them there, see what I can find out when they haul our late friend out of the mud."

Cletus reached over and took a faded Fedora off the top of a particle board world globe bar he kept beside his desk and stuck it on his head at a cocky angle. Reaching to the front breast pocket of his shirt, he pulled free a small stack of cards. He shuffled through until he'd found what he was looking for, then stuck the brightly lettered PRESS card in his hat.

"That guy looked more in need of a priest than a reporter," Jasper commented.

"I'm not a priest," Cletus stood up, indignant. "I follow no Pope. I am a Reverend in the Universal Life Church. We don't perform last rites."

Jasper snorted. "Universal Life my ass. You are a Reverend in the church of send in your ten dollars and a coupon."

"Amounts to the same, in the eyes of the Lord," Cletus replied with a wink. "Folks don't really mind who saves them, as long as they can go on sinning until their cards are punched."

Jasper shook his head, grabbed what remained of his twelve-pack, and headed for the door. "You give me a call, you find out who that guy is. And mind you, don't let them trample over my fishing hole."

"God forbid that the unclean should tread upon the sacred shoreline of mud," Cletus intoned, clapping his hand to his heart. "You have my word as a lover of catfish."

Then Jasper was out the door, and Cletus was close behind, the notebook tucked under one arm. The sun was dropping toward 4:00. Time waited for no man, not even a dead one.

Before he was even out of his driveway, Cletus had his cell phone to his ear and the number one memory button pressed. 911 rang once, then hit a tone and went to a busy signal. Cletus cursed and punched the number again. This time, after a short hesitation, he heard a series of clicks, and he was connected. Two rings and the phone was answered by a slow, sweet woman's voice.

"Hey, Colleen," Cletus cut in, before she could finish her spiel. "It's Cletus. I've got a good one for you."

"Hey Cletus. You shoot another poacher?"

"Nope. Didn't shoot anyone," Cletus assured her. "Yet. I got wind of something you might want to have checked out. Seems there's a man in the swamp off 17 that forgot you need to breathe to socialize in these parts."

"You pulling my leg, Cletus?" Colleen's voice had shifted from friendly to irritated as if handled by a double-clutching dirt-track driver. Cletus grimaced.

"Not at all," he assured her. "Got it on good authority. It's out past the Chester place, about a mile along the bypass. You turn off behind the Coles' barn and curve in around the trees."

"The fishin' hole?" Colleen asked.

Cletus grinned. Jasper thought that place was a secret, but everyone who'd lived in the county in the past twenty years knew the place well enough."

"Exactly," he said.

"I'll get Bob out there," she said with a sigh. "You'd better be tellin' me the truth this time. Bob'll have my ass if there's nothing there."

"I think you might want to call the Troopers," Cletus replied. "I don't think he tripped in the swamp and drowned."

There was a moment's silence, then Colleen continued. "You know I can't do that, Cletus. Bob'd have my hide. If there's something out there, he'll have to find it first, or we'll have hell to pay."

Cletus chuckled. He'd known this, of course. "Just thought it was my civic duty to provide all the facts, and the benefit of my long years of experience" he said. "I'll head over there a little later – give ol' Bob a chance to dig in and set up his "crime scene.""

More silence. "He really tries, you know Cletus? He does. You shouldn't take that attitude with him."

Cletus didn't answer, but his grin widened. Then, before he hung up, he added, "You have yourself a wonderful day, Colleen."

The line went dead, and Cletus pulled back onto the road and headed for the highway.

When Cletus pulled in next to Bob's cruiser, he saw the young officer standing by the shoreline where swamp met the green grass and shrubbery, glaring down into the water. The marshy ground seemed un-intimidated by Bob's stern gaze. Flies buzzed and whirled around his booted feet, occasionally lighting on his face or neck. Cletus watched Bob swat at them in irritation for a few minutes, then he killed the engine and stepped out of his truck.

Cletus didn't speak at first, moving up to stand beside the other man and a little further back from the water. Up closer, he could see that Bob's normally brightly spit-shined boots were caked with slime and mud. His sleeves were rolled up to the elbows, and sweat rolled down his forehead, streaked his cheeks and slid under the top of his collar, where a damp, dark stain was slowly spreading.

On the bank, just as Jasper had described, a man's legs protruded from the water and dangled over the bank. There were scrapes where Bob had apparently been attempting to tug the body free, but it was still submerged from the waist up.

About two feet beyond that point, an odd root formation – or the branches of some long-fallen tree, stretched up out of the muck. That sight, for some reason, itched at Cletus' mind. He nearly stepped back, but at that moment, Bob spoke.

"Hell of a thing," Bob said. He turned, and Cletus saw that something was wrong before the officer's words confirmed it. Bob spoke as if dazed, his voice slipping in from some point very far away.

"Hell of a thing," he repeated. "Just stuck there, Cletus. Won't budge. Like a fishin' line in a bramble patch. Just stuck."

Cletus felt something prickle in the hairs on the back of his neck. He stared down at the water, lapping gently at the shore, then slid his gaze out to that strange root formation. Or was it branches? Something about it was wrong, but Cletus couldn't quite nail it down.

"Let's get him out of there, Bob," Cletus said at last. "The two of us ought to be able to yank him free."

Bob didn't move at first. Cletus could see that the man sensed the "something" that was wrong as clearly as he himself did, and Bob had been standing there longer. Staring. Wondering. He'd had some time, in fact, to worry those thoughts around in his head. Finally, the man nodded.

"Reckon we could at that," he said.

Cletus leaned down slowly, getting a tight, if reluctant grip on one of the booted ankles protruding from the water. Bob leaned in with an equal lack of enthusiasm and gripped the other. Both men drew in deep breaths, steadying themselves for what was to come, then Cletus said, "Now."

They heaved. At first, nothing happened. Cletus strained, and he felt his fingers slipping. He concentrated on not concentrating on the feel of dead, slimy flesh. Beside him, Bob was grunting with his own effort, and it seemed as if it might be for nothing. The dead guy wasn't budging.

Then, all at once, there was a loud sucking sound and Cletus felt the world tilt. The body came free, slid up the bank and sent the two men reeling backward, fighting for balance, and fighting even harder to not be under that wet, rotting mess when it came to rest on the bank. Cletus released his hold on the ankle and lurched to the side, barely managing to keep his balance.

Bob had better luck, to one way of thinking. He was standing off to the other side, an empty, sodden boot in his hand.

The mud must have slicked his skin, Cletus thought absently. It was about then he noticed that Bob wasn't standing still. Bob, in fact, was backing away from the shoreline, taking shaky, uneven steps that grew quicker and less graceful as each moment passed. His arm dropped to his side, and the wet boot brushed his thigh. Bob screamed. Not a yell, or a manly holler, but a scream, full-throated, up from the diaphragm (as Miss Dozier had taught them so many years before) – long, loud and enough to make Cletus' eyes bulge.

Bob tossed the shoe aside like it was a snake, and turned, shooting off toward his squad car like he was chased by a bullet.

"Bob?" Cletus asked, his voice far too soft to be heard. Bob wasn't listening, that was clear enough, in any case.

Then Cletus turned, and perfectly good beer, courtesy of his buddy Jasper, resurfaced as bile and threatened to shoot between his lips in a geyser.

"Jesus Jumping Jehosephat CHRIST" he managed, nearly releasing the bile after all his effort to stop it.

Bob didn't hear him. Bob wasn't there. He'd reached his squad car and was leaning against it heavily, pointedly ignoring the water, Cletus, and the thing that lay on the bank. The thing that had looked so much like a man. The thing that had been wearing flannel and work boots – dead, yes indeed, dead as a doornail – but a man, for all that. The thing that no way in hell was a man. Bob wasn't looking at it, thinking about it, or even believing it, at that moment, but Cletus was doing all those things, and his eyes watered with tears from the stench of it.

Everything was normal up to the shoulders. Big, yes, a strapping, big fellow with bulging, well-muscled arms and a blue tattoo of a cross on the left wrist. Two hands, ten fingers, as close as Cletus could tell, everything inventoried and in order, just as it should be. Except . . . well, except that no man Cletus had ever known had sported an eight point rack. Not even a nub of antler had he witnessed in all the years of his life, other than on four-footed creatures. What lay before him in the muck appeared to be a man, with the head of a white-tail buck, dripping slime, moss and muck into a puddle that dribbled back toward the swamp. Flies flitted around those impossible horns, and slimy weeds trailed down and away behind, back in the direction from which they'd tugged him – it – free.

There was no way to tell where man ended and deer began. The furry neck dipped beneath the sodden flannel collar. The eyes were glazed, milky and beginning to rot. Cletus' stomach churned, but he moved closer in morbid fascination. He had to know – had to see. He leaned in close, holding his breath against the stench, purposefully avoiding the rotting, rheumy eyes staring lifelessly toward the heavens, and gripped the collar of the shirt. He didn't bother with niceties. He gripped, and he yanked, feeling the buttons on the front of the shirt give way with a soft, wet sound. No loud tearing – it just came away revealing the thing's neck.

A ragged line, like a scar, but sloppy and rough, ran around the man's throat. The head attached just at the base of what would have been his neck, rolling down in back toward the muscles of his shoulders and dipping with a "v" of fur down the center of his chest. Everything above that was adult Bambi, abuzz with flies now that it had been dragged free of the water and stared lifelessly into the later afternoon sky.

Cletus turned slowly. Bob leaned against the side of his cruiser. The microphone of his radio dangled loosely from one hand, and his forehead was on his other arm. The man's hair was tangled and matted with sweat, and he wasn't moving. Cletus could hear the radio squawking, and for a moment he wondered if Bob had even called in.

Cletus didn't look back at the water, or the thing in the mud. He walked straight to Bob, watching his own boots carefully as he went, measuring each step by the number of heartbeats pounding in his head between strides. Bob didn't look up as he approached, and Cletus didn't expect it. He knew how Bob felt, and if he stopped for even a second, he'd be leaning on the squad car himself, listening to the radio talk to nobody and waiting for someone to come along and find them.

That wasn't an option. Cletus reached the squad car, and without hesitation, reached down and yanked the microphone from Bob's limp grip. The man didn't even flinch. From inside the squad car, he heard Colleen's distressed voice.

"Bob? Bob? Report please. What the HELL is going on out there Bob?"

Cletus keyed the mic and broke in.

"Colleen? This is Cletus."

Silence for a moment, then, "Cletus? What the hell are you doing on this frequency? Where's Bob?"

"He's right here, Colleen. We have a . . . situation."

More silence.

"Call the troopers, Colleen. Get their asses out here and now. I won't answer any questions, but you're welcome to talk to Bob some more. I don't think he's going to prove very communicative."

Cletus dropped the mic and turned toward his truck. He had a camera in the back, and he needed to get some work done before Colleen quit squawking and did as she'd been told. Bob never moved. Very low, Cletus heard the young officer muttering to himself. It sounded like prayer.

Chapter Two

The Cotton Gin was a low slung club set back from the road and tucked away on a side street just outside Old Mill. At lunchtime, they served up barbecued pork sandwiches and sweet potato fries. In the evening they served up whiskey and beer. Both crowds lined the parking lot with pickups, beat-up sedans, and motorcycles. Cletus pulled in and parked near the rear of the lot, scanning the other vehicles before climbing out for a stretch and a better look.

The regular crowd had arrived early. There were a few trucks Cletus didn't recognize mixed in, mostly with Virginia plates, and one old Mercedes coupe that almost certainly belonged to a salesman. Things in Old Mill didn't change much, and when they did, even the changes were predictable.

As Cletus crossed the gravel lot toward the entrance, he saw a familiar plume of gravel and dust approaching, and he grinned.

"Like a Yellowstone geyser," he said to no one in particular.

A moment later, he stepped aside as a baby blue 1966 Ford Thunderbird rolled into the lot. The paint gleamed, and the wide white walls caught the last of the late afternoon light nicely. The Ford pulled into a spot along the back, near where Cletus himself had parked, and a large, ruddy-faced man sporting a Stetson hat and a prodigious collection of well-digested bear beneath his belt stepped out.

"Evenin', Horton," Cletus called out. He stood and waited as the older man took a look around, then crossed to where Cletus stood.

"Evenin', Cletus. You're here kind of early tonight. Rough day?"

"Actually, Horton," Cletus replied with a grin, "I was hoping I'd run into you."

Actually, hope had nothing to do with it. Every Thursday without fail the local classic auto group met down south in Camden, and Horton was the treasurer. He hadn't missed one of those gatherings in the ten years they'd been going on, and Cletus knew it. He also knew that when the festivities broke up, Horton always came to the Gin.

When he wasn't tooling about the countryside in his T-bird, Horton Buck was the acting Coroner of Perquimans County. Cletus knew the body had gone to Horton first, he'd double checked with Colleen. Once she'd finished telling him how Bob had come in , spent the first half hour in the bathroom wasting what was left of his breakfast, and the rest of the day back out in the swamp with the Troopers, she told Cletus that Horton had been called to pronounce the body dead, and to haul it in to the morgue.

For once, Cletus felt sorry for Bob. He didn't know if he could have kept himself together after what he'd witnessed that morning with a bunch of stiff-necked State Troopers running him around the swamp and asking damned fool questions. Cletus didn't have to hear the questions to know what they were, and he didn't have to be a genius to know that those boys weren't going back to their own headquarters with anything approaching the truth, the whole truth, or anything in that neighborhood. They were going to find the simplest explanation and run with it. They were going to keep it as far from the press as they could, as well as the fine citizens of Old Mill, until they had some idea what they had on their hands.

Horton skirted the bar and headed for the booths in the back. The table furthest from the bar had a small sign on it that read "Reserved." Horton grabbed the sign, placed it in the back of the booth, and spun it around. It now read "Occupied," and he grinned up at Cletus, who slid in across from him with a chuckle and a shake of his head.

"Even the Coroner's Office has its perks," Horton said. "What's on your mind, Cletus?"

"I think you know the answer to that, Hort," Cletus said.

Horton looked at his clasped hands, his already flushed face reddening. A waitress approached them and sat a large pitcher of beer and two glasses between them, then disappeared back into the noise and smoke. They might as well have been sitting behind a wall.

"I can't talk about that Cletus," Horton said. "You know that.

There's lines you don't cross."

"That isn't going to cut it, Hort." Cletus leaned closer for emphasis. "You weren't out there this morning. I was. What I saw...I can't explain it. Hell, I doubt if you can explain it, but I know you know more about it than I do. I need to know what's going on."

"You working this for someone?" Horton asked.

Cletus shook his head. "I told Jasper I'd look into it. I called Bob, and we both went out there. We pulled that...body...out of the swamp. I've never seen anything like it, and I hope I never do again, but damn it Horton, I want to know what the hell it was. I mean, at first it looked like someone had just sewed a head onto a dead body, but just before I left, I got a closer look. I'm no medic, but I've seen cuts, and stitches. Those were healing."

Horton took a long drag on his beer and sat back. He blinked, swallowed, and emptied the glass in the second gulp. He glanced around the bar as if there might be spies lurking in the shadows. Cletus almost laughed, but managed somehow to hold it in. No one in the county, and least of all in The Cotton Gin gave a hoot in Hell what Horton said or thought, and they sure weren't going to break up a good game of eight-ball to eavesdrop on him.

"What do the troopers say?" Cletus asked. "I assume you told them what you'd seen?"

"I tried," Horton said, glowering and taking another swig of beer. "Lord knows. They're already off on a five county hunt for a crazed taxidermist. They plan to question folks with hunting licenses and they're going to contact the FBI to run a search through NCIC. The body is headed to the State Bureau crime lab up in Raleigh. They're hoping for prints."

"You didn't see any?" Cletus asked.

"I asked if they had a double-D Goddam database for hoofprints," Horton snorted, finishing his second glass of beer.

Cletus drained his first. Getting useful information out of Horton was an iffy proposition at the best of times. He hoped the Gin had enough beer.

"So," Cletus said, "we both know that skin was healing. We both know that skin could no way in hell have been healing. We both know men don't come to the Dismal Swamp for head transplants on a regular basis, and, even though the Weekly World News is my Bible, I swear on Bat Boy's honor I've never read of any head transplant that took. Barring the possibility that some rednecked hunter tried his computer scanner on the buck he just shot and 3-D Photoshopped it onto his cousin, you got any ideas?"

Horton looked at Cletus and blinked, then glanced down at his beer glass as if seeing it for the first time. He placed the glass carefully on the table and steepled his hands, looking off across the bar as if Cletus wasn't there at all.

"Most folks," Horton said softly, "think I'm something of an idiot, Cletus," he said softly.

Cletus was taken aback by the comment, but held his silence. He knew he should probably have denied the truth of the statement, but they both knew if he did it would be a lie. Horton saved him the trouble by continuing.

"Fact is, I didn't have to come back to Old Mill at all. Had offers from Raleigh, Richmond up in Virginia, even an outfit out in California. There was a time I was going places, and this wasn't one of 'em. Then I met Clara, and things changed. You knew her folks, didn't you Cletus? Harry and Jenny?"

Cletus nodded. "They took care of me a few times when my pop was out to sea. They were good folks."

Horton nodded. "They were, and Clara? She was my angel. She might have moved with me to Raleigh. She might even have gone to California, but she'd have been miserable the whole time. Her life was here, and my life, as it turns out, was with her. So I stayed. Anyway, there's a point to all of this. I know a thing or two about medicine, and biology, and a bit about wounds.

Cletus had a thousand words on the tip of his tongue, but he kept them to himself. This was a side of Horton he'd never seen, and he had an idea he was about to learn some other things as well.

"I worked with a surgeon once," Horton said, "who specialized in transplants. I learned a lot during that internship. I saw a lot of lives saved, a lot of others lost, and I paid attention. One of the biggest fears in a transplant is that the body will take a perfectly good organ and reject it. Sometimes it happened so fast the patient was dead before they could get them off the operating table. Other times things seemed fine, and then degraded. It was always faster near the end. We know a lot about the human body, but for the most part it's just a game of educated guesses. We save a lot of lives, but every time we operate, we learn something we didn't know before, or we find out that something we thought we knew is bullshit.

"That man you pulled out of the swamp – and he was a man, at least he started out that way – didn't die because the transplant was botched. He didn't die because it was impossible. He died because his body rejected it. Maybe it goes deeper than that. Man of science or not, I like to think there's more to a man than the flesh he carries around with him. Maybe his soul rejected it – who can say. The inflammation around the stitches was something I've seen before. The blood wasn't matched. He tried to live…or something tried to live in that body…but it just couldn't do it, Cletus."

Cletus' skin had gone clammy, and for the second time that day his stomach was on the verge of doing some rejecting of its own.

"What are you saying, Horton? Bottom line?" he asked.

"I'm saying it isn't the fact some psycho doctor out there sewed a damned deer head onto man that scares me, Cletus. It's the fact it almost worked."

Horton stood up very suddenly and turned away from the table. Cletus started to follow, then thought better of it. He didn't know what to say. Horton tottered across the bar, swung wide of the pool table, and headed for the door. When it closed behind him, Cletus was still watching. Then he sat back, poured another beer, and lost himself in his thoughts.

The Gin wasn't busy, but business was steady. Men came and went on their way home from work, or out from home. A local trucking company softball team breezed through, downed several pitchers of beer, and rolled back out. Cletus sat and watched them, and he thought. He watched them because they were all alive, and moving, and if he closed his eyes and quit watching, even for a moment, he heard the wet, sucking sound of swamp mud releasing its hold on those damned antlers, and he saw the jagged line of stitches across the man's chest.

He shouldn't have been sitting and drinking so far from home, and he shouldn't have been spending his time worrying over a dead man, even one sprouting antlers. No one was paying him on this one, and with the State Troopers in charge and the FBI on call, it wasn't likely that Old Mills' finest were going to call him in as a consultant. He had mail-order courses to finish. He had a couple dozen "magic" talismans to mail to fill orders from his advertisement in the latest Weekly World News. There were dozens of more important things he could have been doing, but somehow he couldn't pry his dead ass out of that booth and get to it.

Finally, when things started to get ugly near the pool table, he rose and dropped a ten on the table behind the empty pitcher. When the action moved to the south side of the table, he moved around the left, narrowly avoiding jostling a woman twice his size in blue jeans half her own. In the clear, he breathed a little easier. He glanced toward the door and saw a tall man in a New York Yankees baseball camp slip out the door.

At that moment he heard a loud crack behind him, and he turned, half-expecting he'd been too slow, and that he'd meet a pool cue teeth first. When things got a bit too drunk out, the Gin was famous for what Cletus liked to term "Redneck Olympics." He'd watched them at it more than once, and he knew better than to stick around when things started to run south of sane. The night he'd stayed to watch, five big men, two farmers, a trucker, and a mechanic from down at the Ford dealer put ten bucks apiece on the bar. Sadie, who'd been tending bar that night, had held the money. The game was simple. They each chugged a glass of beer. Whoever took the longest to down his drink was "it". Once this formality was behind them, they turned to the front door.

Whoever walked through that door next, woman, man, sheriff, or Hell's Angel, the man who was "it" had a choice. He could step forward and take a swing, no warning, and no mercy, or he could match the fifty bucks on the bar. If he swung, and knocked whoever it was down, he got the fifty bucks. If he chickened out, or if it was someone's grandmother, and he just couldn't do it, he matched the pot, and they drank again. The night Cletus had watched, they'd matched twice before Amos Lester said "Aw Hell" and swung before the door was even all the way open. He hooked his ham fist around the corner and caught one of three marines who were coming in flush on the jaw. The marine went down, and Amos took his money quick. Then the marine got up.

The Gin was not a watering hole for the weak of heart.

The fight at the pool table had gone past the cursing stage. The big woman he'd missed the opportunity to do the bump with had her pool cue, tip down, gripped like a club, and she was advancing on a big man with so much hair it erupted from the collar of his shirt and spilled over his shoulders. He leaned on the wall, holding his head and screaming. Blood seeped through his fingers.

"Time to go," Cletus muttered. He turned and hurried out into the parking lot, just in time to hear a loud cry for help.

Cletus made a habit of being observant. It was necessary for about half the jobs he performed, and a good idea for the other half. It was the kind of ability that kept you from getting the butt-end of a pool cue up side your head, and that kind of advantage was important.

When he stepped out of the bar, he noticed two things immediately: a ratty old pickup truck hitting second gear, chewing gravel and shooting out of the parking lot and on toward Highway 17; a big man in a t-shirt that failed to reach his belt by four inches running straight at him, screaming and bellowing at the top of his lungs. His belly swung from side to side, and his voice was a harsh blast of air forced past a burning need to breathe; Jasper running his truck into the ditch as the first truck shot past, nearly taking off his rear-view.

"Damn," Cletus said.

He didn't know the fat guy, and he wasn't fast enough on his feet to give chase, so he took off at a run toward Jasper. The big guy saw him, tried to switch direction and met the sad reality of gravity. His back leg caught in the gravel, his front twisted, and he went down. Cletus saw this out of the corner of his eye, but he was too far away to prevent the fall, and about a hundred pounds shy of a serious attempt, so he kept moving.

"Hey!" the man got out one word, and then a sharp cry as he hit the ground, trying in vain to break his fall with his hands. Cletus almost stopped then. He heard the gasp of pain and knew something was likely broken, but just then he caught sight of Jasper, and he went on to the ditch.

Jasper was bent forward over his steering wheel. Cletus couldn't tell if he was moving, but it looked bad. The pickup was buried nose first in the mud at the base of the ditch. It was about four feet down, and Cletus took it at a slide, catching himself on the driver's side door, grabbing the handle and yanking it open. Jasper turned then, dazed, and Cletus saw a trickle of blood on his friend's forehead.

"Take 'er easy Jasper," Cletus said. "Just sit there a minute till I get a chance to look you over."

"Cletus?" Jasper asked.

"Yeah Jaz, it's me," Cletus said. "I was coming out of the bar when that asshole ran you off the road. You get a look at him?"

Jasper shook his head, and his face screwed itself into a pained expression as the stupidity of such a gesture made itself known.

"Didn't get a good look," Jasper said at last. "It's dark, and I was tryin' not to get my ass killed. Funny thing though, Cletus. I didn't see the guy who was driving – but there was a couple fellas in back. I nearly missed the turn when I saw them. I swear they was white – you know – like them Mime assholes you see on TV, or Gene Simmons from Kiss back before they washed their faces. Spooky as hell."

Before Cletus could question him further, the man in the parking lot let out a scream. Cursing, Cletus stepped back from the truck.

"I got to go see if I can help Shamu back there, Jaz. You take it easy till the cops get here."

"No cops, Cletus. I got to get out of here."

"Why in..." Cletus stopped mid-sentence. The floor of the pickup was littered with beer cans.

"Go sit in my truck," he growled. "Can you walk?"

"I think so," Jasper said. "Thanks Cletus."

"'Just get over there. I have to check the guy in the parking lot and get him some help. I also want to find out if he saw anything. Maybe you can find that guy and his to clown-painted friends and get some money to fix your truck."

Cletus spun away and headed back to where the fat guy was flopping in the gravel like a beached salmon. Cletus reached him just as he managed to pull himself back to a seated position.

"Hold on there, Bubbah," Cletus said, putting a hand on the guy's shoulder. "Just stay down there and try not to move 'till we see if all the parts are still where they belong."

The man saw Cletus, and his eyes grew wide. Despite the obvious pain it caused, not to mention damage to the parking lot, he choked out a single word, something that sounded like "llyn" and started back-stroking like a grounded Olympic swimmer.

Cletus stood, dumbfounded, and watched him go.

"What the hell did you say?" he asked.

When there was no coherent answer, Cletus gave chase with a curse.

Chapter Three

"Aliens!"

Cletus stopped in his tracks so fast he nearly lost his balance and joined Bubbah on the ground. He stared, and Bubbah stared. The front door of the bar popped open and one of the bartenders glanced out. He still held a towel in his hand, and he didn't look happy.

Cletus glanced at him, then back at the guy on the ground.

"Calm down, Bubbah," he said, and tell me what you saw.

"My name ain't Bubbah," the guy spit. His lip was still quivering, but as Cletus came fully into carbon-based alcohol fueled life-form focus, he looked a little less crazed. He stared up at Cletus, blinked, and went on.

"My name ain't Bubbah," he repeated, "and you ain't an alien."

"Two for two," Cletus replied. "You want to tell me what the blue Jesus you're talking about?"

"Name's Earl," the guys said. "Earl Suggs."

"Nice to meet you, Earl," Cletus replied. He caught movement out of the corner of his eye and knew that either the bartender, or someone else from the bar, was approaching quickly. "You want to tell me what you were screaming about? And while you're at it, why would you think I was an alien?"

"Abduction," Earl said, as if he hadn't heard Cletus at all. "It was a goddamned abduction, right here at the Gin."

Cletus thought fast. He had about thirty seconds before half the drunken population of The Cotton Gin closed in on the two of them, and after that he probably wouldn't get coherent word out of Earl here.

"Tell you what, Earl," he said. "My name is Cletus Diggs. Sometimes I write stories that get into the Weekly Globe Examiner.

Your alien story might just get you on the front page, if you're interested."

Earl looked interested, but Cletus didn't waste time waiting for an answer.

"You come with me, Earl. My buddy Jasper just wrecked his truck, so the two of you could both use some lookin' after. We'll go back to Jasper's house – his daddy was a medic in the Coast Guard. I'll get you a beer, and you can tell me about the aliens, what do you say?"

Earl blinked, then he glanced over at the small group of drunks trickling out of the bar. He looked back at Cletus.

"You write for the Weekly Globe?"

"Cross my heart," Cletus replied. "I'd swear, but I'm a man of the cloth. It's a long story. You comin' Earl? If those guys catch up with us there's going to be a lot of questions. Now, I believe you, but what do you suppose folks are gonna say if you start yappin' about aliens?"

"But I saw 'em," Earl whined.

Cletus reached down and took the big man by the hand.

"I'm sure you did," he said. "But after what I saw going on inside by the pool table, that crowd isn't going to be your target audience. Best get movin', Earl."

Earl glanced a final time at the door, then nodded, gripped Cletus' hand, and hauled himself to his feet. He nearly crumpled, and Cletus caught him, slipping under Earl's shoulder and bracing for shock.

"It's my ankle," Earl said. "Twisted it when I fell."

Cletus didn't answer. He just turned and started across the parking lot toward his truck with Earl limping along at his side. The crowd from the bar stopped to watch them go. A couple of good old boys took a few more steps in pursuit, but apparently the call of beer was too strong. By the time Cletus helped Earl up to the side of the truck, and Jasper opened the door for them.

"Jasper," Cletus said, "Meet Earl. Earl Suggs. Mr. Suggs saw the folks who ran you off the road."

Jasper helped haul Earl up onto the seat beside him. Cletus stepped round and clambered in behind the wheel.

"We're headed back to your place," Cletus said. "You got beer?"

"Pap brought home a case just this morning," Jasper replied. "There ought to be a few left."

Cletus stared at his friend.

Jasper stared back.

"What?" he asked. "We like beer, okay? No law against that."

"Nothing, Jasper. I was just thinking maybe if you'd had a few less beers, your truck might still be rolling under your ass, instead of nose deep in that ditch back there."

"I ain't drunk," Jasper said, blustering. "I only had…"

"They was aliens," Earl cut in. "In that truck? Aliens. Guy in front was all covered in some sort of black coat. He had a hat pulled down low. Those other two, though, they had their faces pressed against the window. I know they saw me. That guy wasn't from around here, but he didn't deserve to be abducted by no aliens."

Jasper fell silent and stared. Cletus kept his eyes directed at the road and fought back the urge to grin. Whatever Jasper did, and Cletus had an idea or two on what that might be, Cletus himself could not afford to seem anything but sincere. He had no idea why he was keeping after this case, but since he was, he needed every advantage he could wrangle.

When Jasper remained silent, Cletus jumped in quick.

"Earl here saw the truck that ran you off the road, Jasper. He also saw them grab a man out of the parking lot at The Gin. He was going to describe them to me, and I figured I'd take some notes and get something off to the Weekly Globe. I'm sure we'll need to get down what you saw too."

"They got meetings for this," Earl cut in. His breath was still a little ragged, and Cletus thought his ankle was hurting like a son of a bitch. "Every week, they got meetings down at the Dreaming Dragon Tattoo parlor. They bring in speakers – people who've been abducted. One day they brought a speaker from the CIA … well… ex-CIA. He worked out there in Arizona at Area 51."

Jasper turned to Cletus.

"What the hell is he talkin' about Cletus? You want me to give him beer? Sounds like he's had a few too many already."

"I think he saw what he saw," Cletus answered slowly. If it hadn't been such a long shot, he'd have hoped Jasper would catch the tone in his voice and play along.

"The hell you say," Jasper said. "You think I was run off the road by aliens and some guy dressed up like Alex Baldwin in that movie "The Shadow" was behind the wheel. Tell me somethin' Cletus. Just when did aliens start abducting folks with pickup trucks instead of saucers?"

"Might've been a saucer," Earl cut in helpfully. "Could have been using a cloaking device. I seen one of them on Star Trek."

Cletus bit down hard on his lip and kept driving.

"Let's get us that beer," he said. "God knows, I need one."

They turned off highway 17 toward The Great Dismal Swamp. In the distance, back in the direction of The Cotton Gin, sirens cut through the night.

Back at Jasper's Pap's farm, they circled the coffee table in the sparsely furnished living room and broke out the beer. Both Jasper and Earl drank deep, but Cletus sat back and sipped his. When he figured things were as calm as they were likely to get, he cleared his throat and sat up.

"First things first," he said. "Earl, you were the first one of us to see that truck. You remember anything about it? Color, scratches, dents, bumpers stickers?"

"Did it glow green and whistle like on the Jetsons," Jasper offered. "Or maybe it just sort of phased in – like from the transporter deck?"

"Shut up, Jaz," Cletus snapped. "This may be a lot more serious than you think."

Earl didn't look upset. It appeared that it might not be the first time he'd been scoffed at, and possibly Jasper wasn't even the best who'd tried. His brow was furrowed, and he was thinking hard.

"You gonna write it down?" he asked at last. Cletus, who'd had the forethought to pull the small spiral notebook he kept in his hip pocket, and a stub of pencil, nodded solemnly.

"It was black," Earl said. "Black as night. I remember thinking it was strange, because it wasn't shiny black, like you'd expect. It was kind of dull."

"Like primer?" Cletus asked.

Earl frowned, then nodded. "Maybe, yeah."

"You didn't notice anything else strange about it?" Cletus asked.

"Nope," Earl said. "Not the truck – just looked like all the others in the lot. That guy came out of the bar and sort of staggered across the parking lot right when I was headed in. He walked past me, skinny fella with short hair, like a sailor – or maybe Coast Guard. He was parked right next to 'em."

"You see any flashing lights?" Jasper cut in.

Cletus glared at him, but Earl only took another long swig of beer.

"So," Cletus said, "We have a flat black pickup and a guy from out of town. Did you see what happened?"

"It was pretty quick," Earl said. "I didn't have any reason to care about that guy. The only reason I looked back was that I heard a crunch of metal. It was the door of the truck. They slammed it open and cracked it into that guy and his car. The two in back – the ones with the white faces? – they jumped outta the back quicker'n greased pigs. They had him up and was draggin' him into the back seat before I really knew what I was seeing. I started after them, but the driver had 'er in gear before I made two steps. They drove right at me. That's when I yelled and started running."

"Sounds like a good plan," Jasper commented. For the first time he didn't sound sarcastic.

"I turned once," Earl said. "I wanted to see if they was really gonna hit me, so I looked over my shoulder and that's when I saw 'em. The driver was all dressed in black. He had one of those black hats that looks sorta like a stetons, but not so big."

"Fedora," Cletus offered.

"Yep, that's it," Earl agreed. "I couldn't see him at all. Saw them others though. Faces white as snow. They had their faces pressed to the glass of the back window, all smushed up. Ain't never seen a man looked like that. Had to be aliens."

A loud "pop" sounded from the kitchen door, and they turned, startled.

Jasper's Pap stood there, staring at them over a beer, his eyes narrowed. "Black pickup and white faces, huh? Don't sound like aliens to me. Sounds like them two boys out Eternity way. Cain't remember their names, but I've seen 'em down town a couple of times. White as sheets and odd as a three dollar bill."

Pap burped then, and turned to Jasper. "You gonna sit there like a lump all night, or you turnin' on Smackdown?"

Cletus stood up, chugged his mostly full beer, and waved.

"I'd love to stay," he said. "Supposed to be a hell of a cage match in the main event, but I have some things I have to take care of. Earl, you need a ride back to your truck?"

"Smackdown's on?" Earl asked.

Jasper was already reaching for the remote. "Yep."

"Mind if I watch?" Earl asked.

Jasper looked at Papa, who shrugged. "I'm gonna have to go down sometime after midnight and tow my truck outta that ditch when the sheriff ain't around. You can ride with me."

Pap went for three fresh cans of beer, and Cletus headed for the door.

"You gonna get me in the Globe?" Earl called after him.

"When I finish the story," Cletus said, turning back with a wink, "you'll be the first to hear."

"Don't forget them aliens!" Earl bellowed.

Cletus paid no attention. On the way to his car, he pulled out his cell phone and dialed the sheriff's office. Colleen answered.

"Get Bob on the line," Cletus said.

"He isn't taking calls, Cletus. Not since he got back this morning, and the troopers took over. Hasn't been out of his office, not to eat, not for coffee. I'm worried."

Cletus stopped by his truck and stared back down toward the highway.

"I'll be right there, Colleen. If he comes out, don't let him leave. Me and ol' Bob have to go on an alien hunt. You can tell him that."

He disconnected the call before she could question him or protest, climbed in behind the wheel of his pickup, and pointed it toward Old Mill.

Chapter Four

When Cletus reached the Sheriff's Office, Colleen waved him past her desk toward the inner office door.

"You aren't going to page him?"

"He wouldn't answer. Hasn't been out of there since just after lunch. I'm worried about him, Cletus."

"He'll be okay, Colleen. You didn't see what we saw."

"You didn't lock yourself in an office and pout," she pointed out.

"Well, that's me," Cletus said. "I've seen a lot of strange things. Hell, I've seen Jasper eat barbecue. Takes a lot to faze me."

"Well, I hope you can get him out of there. We've got three calls and Lester's running his butt off trying to handle it all."

"I'll see what I can do," Cletus said.

He turned to the inner office door, knocked once, and pushed it open.

Bob sat behind his desk, turned to face the one window in the office. The blinds were pulled down tight, and the curtains were drawn. A single small desk lamp provided the only illumination. An empty coffee cup sat on the desk blotter.

"Hey, Bob," Cletus said.

Bob said nothing, and Cletus stepped closer.

"You okay?" he asked.

For a moment it seemed Bob would remain silent; then he spoke.

"What the hell kind of question is that, Cletus?" he asked. "You saw that thing. Hell, we both had it by the boots."

"That's true," Cletus said. "Whatever it was, though, it's gone now. I don't expect we're going to find too many more like it."

"Shouldn't have been even one," Bob said. He didn't so much speak the words as spit them. "How can I go out there, Cletus? How can I know? What if I pull over a speeder out on 17, walk up to the driver's side window, and see antlers through the glass? What if it's something else? Something worse?"

Bob's hand shook. Cletus had seen the onset of panic before, and he knew he had to stop it quick, or it might get ugly.

"Then you give Bambi a ticket and get on with your life," he said. "What are you doing, Bob? We got a dead man on his way to Raleigh, and he was killed right here. Troopers are out scouring the county for crazed taxidermists, and here you sit. You think it was some guy got tired of mounting heads on his wall and decided to use his brother-in-law instead?"

"No," Bob said flatly. "I don't think it was a taxidermist. I don't think it was a hunter. I pray to God it wasn't anyone from Old Mill at all, but there you go, Cletus. He was in the damned fishing hole. Our fishing hole. Someone dropped him there, and whoever it was is a hell of a lot crazier than anyone I've run across in my short but illustrious career as Sheriff."

"Okay," Cletus answered slowly. "I think that's a fair assessment. Now what are you going to do about it?"

Bob turned. He glared up at Cletus through tired, sunken eyes, his teeth gritted.

"Do?" he said. "DO? Nothing, Cletus. What is there to do? We found him, State Investigative Service took him, and the troopers are currently running all our buddies in because they have a lifetime subscription to the Herter's Fish and Game catalog in their den and half-assed jackrabbit mounts on their Tiki bars. There isn't a damned thing I can do…why the hell you think I'm sitting in here?"

Cletus met Bob's gaze levelly.

"I think you're sitting in here on your ass because you're scared of what you might find if you don't. You know as well as I do there's someone out there more than a bubble off plumb, you going to let him get someone else? You going to trust those troopers to do your job? They don't know folks here, and they don't know the swamp. They might be the only men in the county that didn't know where the fishin' hole was before we told them. They aren't going to find this guy, so maybe we'd better."

"We?" Bob said.

"We," Cletus agreed. "We need to get going, Bob. We need to get you some food, and some rest. Tomorrow morning we need to take a spin out to Eternity."

"Now who's a bubble off?" Bob asked. "Eternity? Just why in hell would we go to Eternity."

"Aliens." Cletus said solemnly. "I'll fill you in on the way."

Bob stared up at him, blinked, then shook his head.

"Fine, but you're buying the food."

Cletus grinned, turned, and leaned out the door, giving Colleen thumbs up. Moments later he and Bob were headed through the outer office in search of food. Colleen frowned, staring at the pile of call slips on her desk.

"Tell Lester I'll make it up to him," Bob told her. "Al will be in in a couple of hours, and I'm in no shape to be making house calls. We'll sort it out tomorrow…right after Cletus and I get back from Eternity."

"Tell St. Peter I said hey," Colleen replied, popping her gum.

Chuckling, Cletus followed Bob out into the darkness, trying not to stare into the shadows.

When Bob pulled up in front of Cletus' trailer the next morning, he had had two tall cups of strong black coffee from Muddy Waters over in Elizabeth City, and his color was back. Whatever he'd thought, dreamed, or told himself when the lights went out must have worked.

Cletus climbed into the Land Rover beside him and took one of the coffees gratefully.

"Dancing Goat," Bob said. "It's Friday's special. Damn good coffee."

Cletus nodded.

"So," Bob said. He pulled a quick U-turn in the driveway and headed back toward the road. "You going to tell me why we need to go to Eternity? I haven't been there more than a couple of times in my life, and both times I got out as quick as I could. Now you tell me because we find a corpse with a deer's head, we should go to Eternity to chase aliens, and for some reason I can't help but take you seriously."

"Well," Cletus began, "maybe not aliens. Albinos though."

He quickly filled the sheriff in on what had happened the night before outside The Cotton Gin, and later at Jasper's place. Bob listened carefully, and when Cletus was done, he nodded.

"I think Jasper's Pap is right," he said. "The only albinos I've ever heard of around these parts are those two boys. It might not have anything to do with our deer man, but if they abducted someone from the Gin, we'd best get out there and see what's what."

"There's more," Cletus said.

Bob turned right, away from Highway 17 and on toward the swamp.

"I'm listening," he said.

"I went on the Internet last night," Cletus said. "I knew I'd seen something about those boys, but I couldn't remember what it was. They went away a few years back. Seems the two of them are some sort of geniuses. Studied medicine, genetics, and a few others things. The papers up in Raleigh tried to make a big deal of it, but neither boy would give them an interview. Later that year, the two disappeared. No one could figure out what happened. All the reporters could turn up was a single picture of the two of them sort of glaring at a camera. It was strange enough I considered finding them myself and doing something for the Weekly Observer, but I never did get around to it.

"To tell you the truth, Eternity pretty much creeps me the hell out."

"It's no vacation spot," Bob agreed.

They drove in silence for a few miles, and Cletus pulled a spiral notebook from his hip pocket. He'd made a few notes. His experience with Eternity was pretty limited, and even Jasper's Pap, when Cletus called up to question him, didn't have much. The town had been rotting into the swamp until a certain Reverend Eli Dozier rolled into town, and ever since then every story that rolled out of the rumor mill was strange.

Eternity wasn't so much a town as a gathering place. There was no store, no gas station, no post office, and there sure as hell were no street lights. There were a couple of warehouses just off the highway for crops, cotton, and supplies, but in Eternity, NC, there was only one thing that mattered. Eternity had a church, and despite the fact that you could spend a week of Sundays walking up and down their one stretch of road without seeing a soul, the pews of that church were full every time the altar candles were lit. The walls gleamed with fresh white paint, and the tin roof was water tight and shone in the sun.

There were a lot of families in and around the outskirts of the Great Dismal Swamp. Some of them have lived there all their lives; others have migrated in as civilization ran them out of older homes and deeper shadows. Freeways, cities, towns and farms surround that land on all sides. Some were on the run from something, or someone – others just wanted to be swallowed up and forgotten.

Bob drove slowly and carefully, weaving the Land Rover around large potholes. Once Cletus had to get out and drag a fallen log out of the road. When he climbed back in, he turned to Bob with a frown.

"You remember any wind last night, Bob?" he asked. "I don't remember seeing any branches down near Old Mill."

"It was clear," Bob replied.

"Someone put that log there, then," Cletus said. "Someone didn't want anyone coming in here today. You think maybe they were afraid they were seen?"

"Could be," Bob replied. He glanced over his shoulder at the shotgun hanging behind the seat. "Someone back here doesn't want to be found, it's likely they're not going to be. I figure we'd better try and track down that preacher. He'll know what's going on if anyone does, and he might be able to lead us to those boys."

Cletus frowned.

"Might be you're right, Bob, and I'll be damned if I can think of a better plan, but I haven't heard anything good about this preacher, Dozier. Things have always been close and quiet out here, but since he came in and started preaching at the church the stories I've heard sound more like something off The Twilight Zone. If there's something going on here, he'll know it alright, but he might be the one behind it as well."

"Yep, figured that too," Bob agreed. "We'll have to be careful with him, for sure, but I don't see us getting anywhere out here unless we go to him first."

The road they were on grew steadily worse as it turned in under the trees, then ran along the bank of the swamp. Cattails shot up from the ditch, and a sheen of green, greasy slime coated the stagnant water. Cletus saw a couple of frogs hit that water. They dipped through the muck and the surface went flat. No ripples. A Water Moccasin slithered off the road and into the ditch.

Bob reached for his radio and pressed the key on his mic.

"Four-One to base," he said. He waited a moment, then tried again. There was a crackle of static, and then – faintly – Colleen's voice came across the speaker.

"Got you weak and barely readable, Four-One, over."

"We're getting ready to pull into Eternity," Bob said, speaking quickly, as if afraid of losing their one contact with the outside world. "This might be related to a kidnapping last night over at The Gin. Stay close to your radio – if we find anything, we'll be calling for backup."

There was another crackle that might have been an answer, but there was no way to be certain. Bob glared at the microphone in his hand, jammed it back onto its holder, and turned his attention to the road.

They rounded the final curve and suddenly the ground beneath their tires was even and free of ruts. The road leading into Eternity was clear and smooth. The trees opened up into a large clearing, and at the far end of that clearing stood the First Church of Light and Starry Wisdom. Neither man had known it was called that, but that was what the large, hand-lettered sign beside the walk leading to the front door proclaimed. It was even spelled correctly.

The parking lot was paved with smooth river stones, and it was empty. There was no sign of a black pickup truck, or any other vehicle. The front door of the church was closed.

"You think anyone's home?" Cletus asked. "Damn place looks like it dropped here out of the clouds."

"It's weird all right. What the hell kind of beliefs you reckon they have in The Church of Light and Starry Wisdom, Cletus? You're the preacher, right? I've heard of about ten flavors of Baptists, Methodists, those fellas that go to church on Saturday, Catholics, hell, we got more churches in Old Mill than we have houses – but I've never heard of anything like this."

"It's a new one on me too, Bob," Cletus said. "I'll look into it when we get back."

Bob pulled in and parked near the door. They sat for a moment, then Cletus took a deep breath, opened his door, and stepped out.

His boots crunched on the gravel. Bob followed, and they headed straight up the walk to the front door of the odd structure. The walls were constructed of rough hewn wood. Hand cut. Cletus thought about that, and he hesitated at the top of the steps, reaching out to run his fingertips over the surface.

"This is all handmade," he said at last. "I figured they must have run some supplies in from Virginia, or out of the county, but I'll be damned if they didn't cut this and shape it by hand. You ever seen wood cut like that, Bob?"

Bob didn't answer. He pulled the heavy flashlight off his belt and rapped the base of it on the wooden door sharply. Cletus fell silent, and they waited. There was no answer, and Bob smacked the door again, then shrugged. He grabbed the door handle, pushed on the latch, and it swung inward easily. Bob followed it through, and Cletus followed.

The light inside had a greenish tinge. There were no stained glass windows like the ones at the Methodist Church in Old Mill, but something had been done to the glass. It didn't look quite clear, nor was it colored. It was as if it had been soaked in something green and become infected. Cletus kept his mouth shut, because he knew it hadn't been that many hours since Bob had been ready to panic. No sense vocalizing the fact the entire place felt diseased, or that the light felt like it was crawling over his skin. Didn't really pay to be thinking about it either.

Cletus turned and stared at the altar. He tried to imagine standing behind that podium, staring out at the rough-hewn pews, his hand on a Bible and his mind on messages from God. The images wouldn't come. The place drew goose bumps from his flesh like pie drew flies, and there was a smell he couldn't quite make out that added to his unease. None of it made him feel closer to God.

"There's a door behind the altar," Bob said.

Cletus followed Bob's gaze. He wasn't at all sure he wanted to know what was behind that door, but there didn't seem to be many choices.

"Let's do it then," he said.

The two of them rounded the altar, and Bob reached out to knock on the door. He stopped just short, frowned, and gripped the knob, turning it and giving it a shove.

"Police," He called, stepping through. Cletus noticed Bob's hand resting near the butt of his gun. Normally he'd have thought it was an overreaction, but at that moment it felt like grabbing a marshmallow to throw at a bear.

They entered a short hall single file. Bob never hesitated; he opened the door on their left. It was a storage closet. He gave it cursory glance, closed the door, and opened the door on the right. He stepped inside, and Cletus followed close behind him.

The room was an office, furnished simply with a desk, a couple of chairs, a small table, and a window overlooking the swamp. There were a couple of papers on the desk, weighted down with a worn bible. There was a bookshelf filled with odd, leather-bound books. They didn't look to Cletus like the standard commentaries on the gospels, or the sermons of any long-dead preacher.

"We'd better check out back," Bob said.

Cletus nodded. He stepped closer to the bookshelf and leaned down. As he did, the sound of a door closing nearly scared him out of his jeans. He fell forward, banging his head on the bookshelf and jostling one of the leather-bound volumes free. It fell at his feet, but he didn't lean to pick it up. He turned.

Bob had his hand on the butt of his gun, but somehow resisted the urge to draw the weapon. Cletus had pushed the door nearly closed after they entered so he could see behind it. It opened, and a man stepped through. He was tall with dark, wavy hair tumbling out from beneath a black fedora. Despite the heat, he wore a suit jacket, also dark. His face was shadowed by the brim of the hat, but Cletus thought he could see eyes glowing in the shadow.

The man stared at them, then tipped his hat back and smiled. It wasn't a happy smile, or a friendly smile. It was the kind of smile Cletus associated with the villain in every dark movie he'd ever watched.

"Reverend Dozier?" Bob asked.

The man nodded.

"Reverend Eli Dozier at your service. Is there something I can do for you gentlemen?"

Cletus was glad Bob was with him at that moment. The sheriff pulled himself together nicely, never missing a beat, and it gave Cletus a chance to lean down, pick up the book he'd knocked off the shelf, and slide it back into place. He got a good glance at the cover, and nearly cursed.

"It's been a while since I've been out here," Bob said. "I thought I might check and see if everything was quiet. We had a bit of trouble last night over to the Cotton Gin in Elizabeth City. Got a report the fellows involved might have headed out your way. Don't suppose you noticed anything out of the ordinary?"

Dozier's serpent's grin widened.

"Can't say that I have, Sheriff," he replied. "We don't see much of anyone or anything out this way, except on Sundays. There being only one road, though, it's hard to figure how we could have missed them."

"My thought exactly," Bob said. "You sure you didn't see a black pickup come out this way last night, or hear it? Report said there might have been a couple of boys in the back seat with white faces. No circus around, so I thought of those twins."

"Twins?" Dozier said. He twisted his face in an almost comical expression of confusion, but just before he did it, Cletus saw him start. It was only a tiny, fleeting crack in the man's weird armor, but Cletus thought Bob had caught it too.

"Anyone else out here said they didn't know about one of the families in your congregation, Reverend, I might tend to believe them. Never seen such a close-in crowd as folks here in Eternity, but I'd appreciate it if you didn't insult my intelligence. There can't be more than a couple pairs of albino twins in the history of this great country."

"Oh, you mean David and Weston," Dozier said smoothly. "The Calhoun boys. Quite the story, those two. Might be the only boys out of Eternity this century with college educations, for all the good it did 'em."

"What do you mean?" Bob asked.

"Well, they're back here, aren't they?" Dozier asked bluntly. "That doesn't qualify in my book as much of a success story. Haven't seen hide nor tail of 'em since they got back. It's like they drove on out of here, went to school, then melted right back into the swamp."

"They don't attend services?" Cletus asked. It was the first time he'd spoken, and he hoped that coming out of left field might catch Dozier off guard, but the man just smiled.

"Their ma and pa come to church every Sunday," he said. "I haven't seen the boys. They weren't big on worship even before they left – I suppose they learned new things to spend their souls on up in Raleigh. What do you think, Cletus?"

Cletus stopped and stood very still. He had never met Dozier in person, and hearing his name come from the man's lips took him by surprise.

"Just one man of the cloth to another," Dozier added. "You think those boys found something new to worship?"

Cletus turned, surveyed the bookshelf behind him, then glanced out at the swamp through the green tinted windows.

"Wouldn't say it surprised me if they did at that," he replied.

Dozier looked like he might chuckle at this, then he bit it back and grimaced.

"If that's all you needed, Sheriff," he said, "I have some things to attend to."

While Bob made a show of writing some notes in the small notebook he carried in his breast pocket, Cletus continued to stare out the window. There was a single bed of flowers halfway to the tree line and the swamp beyond, and there was something strange about it. He took half a step closer to the window and concentrated, but just then Bob laid hand on his shoulder, startling him.

"We'd best be going, Cletus," he said. "We have a few more stops to make on the way back. I want to see if any other folks out here might have seen that truck."

Cletus nodded, frowning, then he turned back to Dozier.

"One other thing," he said. "The guy driving that truck last night? He was wearing a dark jacket and a fedora. You know anyone fits that description, Reverend?"

Dozier's eyes narrowed until they were nothing but dark slits, and he dipped his chin so the brim of his hat shielded his expression. He didn't answer, and Cletus turned, leading the way back to the church, and out into the parking lot.

"He knows something," Cletus said.

Bob nodded. "We'll talk about it after we get clear of here."

"Don't have to tell me twice," Cletus muttered.

They climbed into the truck and Bob gunned the engine, cutting twin ruts in the carefully tended drive. Cletus looked into the side mirror. Reverend Dozier was watching them go. He was standing directly in front of the odd little flower bed. From that distance, he looked like a scarecrow, or some sort of weird, swamp wraith.

Then they rounded the corner, and the church was out of sight.

Chapter Five

Cletus waited until they were clear of the swamp, leaving Bob to concentrate on negotiating the bumpy, unpaved road.

"You see that book I knocked off the shelf?" he finally asked. "The one I was trying to pick up when he came through the door?"

Bob turned and glanced at him, the focused on the road.

"Nope. Why?"

"I don't know what it was, exactly," Cletus said, "but I can tell you one thing. The front cover was tooled leather. It didn't have a title, but there was a pretty good likeness of a man with a seven point rack burned in deep."

Cletus saw Bob's knuckles whiten as he gripped the steering wheel too tightly. The sheriff's mouth tightened in to a grim line, but at first he didn't speak. He turned off onto the feeder road and pointed the Land Rover toward Highway 17.

"There's more," Cletus said. This time he didn't look at Bob, but stared out at the road. "There was something wrong with that flower bed out in back of the church."

"The flower bed?" Bob asked. "You had a problem with their flower bed, Cletus?"

"You didn't get a good look at it," Cletus said. "I did. You see any other flowers in Eternity, Bob?"

The silence was all the answer Cletus needed.

"There weren't any other flowers. One, single bed, in a circle, halfway from the church to that back line of trees. There was something sticking up out of the middle. I might have figured out what it was, but Dozier walked in."

"What are you thinking?" Bob asked.

"Don't know," Cletus admitted. "I mean, hell, Bob, it could be a very small graveyard, or some weird shrine. There might have been a well there and they grew flowers around it to keep folks from stepping into it and drowning. It was strange as hell, and when you peeled out of that parking lot, Dozier was standing right beside that flower bed, watching like he was waiting for us to be out of sight."

Bob was quiet for a while after that, and Cletus watched traffic passing. As they turned down the road toward Cletus' place, Bob broke the silence again.

"So, what you think I should do, Cletus?"

There was no 'we' – and Cletus wasn't sure how he felt about that. He didn't really want anything more to do with Dozier, or Eternity, and he damn sure didn't want to pull anymore of Bambi's evolved cousins out of the swamp, but he didn't think he'd be able to sleep until they put an end to it. Maybe not then.

"I'm not sure," he said. "I don't think anyone's going to give you a warrant because I thought a flower bed was weird. You tell the states boys about that book I saw, you might get them to swarm the place.

"We could go back," Bob said. He didn't turn to meet Cletus' gaze, and his fingers were white on the steering wheel again, but his expression was one of tight determination.

"And stake out the posies?" Cletus asked, then immediately felt like a jerk. He'd been hoping Bob would keep him in the game, and now that the door was open he showed his customary lack of tact.

"We go back," he added, "we need us a plan, Bob. We also need to know more about what we're getting into."

"You got any ideas how we'll do that?" Bob asked. "I don't reckon we'll find the good citizens of Eternity too forthcoming. Fact is, I'm not sure I can find any of them at all. The only time they come out of the woodwork is on Sunday, and I don't think they'd take kindly to my stepping up to the altar to ask them questions."

"And that's four days away," Cletus added. "If that guy they took from the Cotton Gin is alive, I'm betting he won't be by Sunday. At least, not like he was, if you know what I mean."

Apparently Bob did. His complexion paled, and he rolled his window down a bit. Cletus was afraid the man was going to spew out into the driveway, but Bob got himself under control.

"I've got to go in and take my shift," Bob said. "I'm going to have to run in some drunks, settle a few home disputes, and break up a fight or two down at the Gin. I don't know if I can do that, but I'm going to try."

Cletus nodded.

"I'm going back to Jasper's place," he said. "I think his pap might be able to get me in touch with someone who understands Eternity, and the swamp, a lot better than I do. I'm also going to hit the Internet and find out what I can about horned men and Reverend Eli Dozier. If we're lucky, I'll find enough to convince someone with more firepower than we have at our disposal to hit that place like a scud missile. If not, we'll have to go back there and get some evidence on our own."

"Hell with that," Bob said. "We'll get us a posse – unofficial, of course. We can get Jasper, maybe his pap, and how 'bout that other guy who thinks he saw a truck full of aliens?"

Cletus snorted laughter and shook his head. "I expect we could get the lot of them," he said. "Can't say I'd feel any safer for it, but you may be right. We'd better take as many as we can get, and we'd better make sure someone knows where we are, and why. I'm thinking it might be a long time before anyone thought to come out toward Eternity to look for us."

He climbed out, and Bob backed the Land Rover up and turned back toward 17. Cletus didn't envy the man the next few hours. Old Mill could be bad enough on a good day – this wasn't one of those. When the trail of dust reached the end of his drive, Cletus climbed into his trailer. He fired up the beat up, stained, old Mr. Coffee, and then the computer, watching the screen roll through its boot procedure to a backdrop of hissing, dripping, liquefied caffeine.

While he waited, he grabbed his phone and punched in Jasper's number. Cletus knew better than to tell his old friend there was work to do. Instead of an answer, he got the whirring hiss on the line that signaled Jasper's Pap's gen-yoo-ine vintage reel to reel answering machine. The thing was a dinosaur, but Pap refused to let it go.

"I bought that thing brand new," he always said. "Found it nice and shiny on the shelves down at Woolworth's. Took me and Emma a year to figure out how to get it to answer the phone, and another six months to figure out what to put on the message. We used to sit around and watch the ding dang thing, ignoring calls and waiting for it to kick in and tell folks we was in the shower, or gone to Outer

Mongolia in search of inner."

Cletus had been hearing the story of that damned machine for nearly thirty years, and it still brought him a chuckle if he thought about it too long. And the damned thing still worked. There was no way to argue with that – quality belonged to things of the past – an archaic term bandied about far too often and with far too little merit in modern times.

The phone's speaker crackled, and pap's voice came onto the line, wavering slightly from the stretched, aged tape it had been recorded onto.

"You've reached Jasper and his pap. Leastways, you'd have reached them if they was here. When you hear this contraption beep, leave a number. If it still plays when I see the light flashing, I'll call you back."

Cletus left a message for Jasper to get some beer and get over to the trailer. He told him to bring pap along if he was up to it, and asked if ol' Earl the alien hunter had left a number, or any way they could reach him to 'follow up' on the story. He didn't say anything about the sheriff, or Eternity, Reverend Dozier, or aliens.

Satisfied, he hung up, stood up, and poured a cup of strong, black coffee. He carried it to his desk, brushed the nearest piles of paper away from his keyboard, and logged onto his computer. Unlike his trailer, and the surface of his desk, his computer screen was almost bleak in its absolute order. He had folder icons lined up on the desktop that held his current projects. He had a hard drive full of the last year's files, and others he planned to follow up on. He also had a complex and nearly paranoid system of backups. Information was the central hub of his life, and he guarded what he had fanatically.

He glanced at his e-mail, saw the box was full of unread messages, missives, requests, and adds for cheap, Internet Viagra. Apparently, Abba Contiga Brezhnev, Contessa of some country he'd never heard of, had a few million bucks she needed laundered, and had gone straight past hello and howdy-do and on to calling him her dear. Nothing earth shattering, and he closed the program with a grunt. Time to get serious.

"Google don't fail me now," he muttered, and between sips of hot, black coffee, he set to work.

Chapter Six

The moon was almost full, and it trickled through the trees like luminous spider silk. The water at the swamp's edge lapped over an old log and sucked at the mud hungrily. In the moonlight, the wet surface beyond the log looked black and slick like an ebony mirror. There were no ripples, and though, very faintly, the screeching song of tree frogs scratched at the air, the silence felt eerie and complete.

A flash of white passed between two trees, and then again. Shadows crossed the grass, as though a huge tree had bent down to touch the earth. The buck stepped into the clearing carefully. He raised his head and sniffed the air. The moonlight caught the clear pools of his eyes, and glimmered on the felt tips of his antlers. He was huge, strong, wary – and thirsty. After a long hesitation, he moved in closer to the water.

He stopped at the edge of the water and shivered, as if he'd felt something crawl through the fur on his back, or a breeze had cut through to chill his skin. Then, slowly, he bent, and he drank.

In the trees behind him, two pale eyes appeared. A few feet further along the tree line, a second set flickered into view as silently as the first. The buck stiffened, as if he'd heard, or sensed something, but when there was no sound, he returned his attention to the water, lapping it up greedily.

In the trees, a woman stood, watching the animal drink. Very slowly, she raised a bow, keeping it parallel to the tree trunks. The buck shivered again, but otherwise seemed not to hear. The woman didn't smile. Her face was blank, like the surface of the water. With the same, slow, silent deliberation she pulled a thin arrow from a quiver dangling over her shoulder and resting against her back. The shaft of the arrow was very narrow, like a willow branch. She notched it to the bow and stood, still as stone, waiting.

The buck finished drinking and lifted its head. As it turned and slowly scanned the clearing, she sighted in on its chest and drew back on the string. Her arm didn't tremble, and there was no creak of bent wood, or thrum of the bow string. She hesitated only a moment, and then, with a whispered word too soft to be heard, she released.

The arrow shot across the clearing. The buck, fast as he was, barely had time to lift his head, eyes starting to roll back in their sockets, before the arrowhead dug into its flesh. The animal reared then, pawing at the air and screaming. The woman stood very still, watching calmly. The arrow was too small for killing – too narrow, and without a lethal tip. The tranquilizer it had been dipped in was more powerful.

The buck leaped for the trees. It was strong, and that first leap carried it across the clearing. As its front hooves struck the soft earth, its legs crumpled beneath it, and it fell forward, rolling hard. He tried to struggle back to his feet, but was only able to raise itself a foot or so before falling heavily on its side.

The woman was out of the trees in seconds, cradling the animal's huge head in her lap. She avoided a final flip of the antlers, stroking the buck's nose and staring down into the wild, fear-soaked depths of its eyes. Others slipped from the forest then. First was a slender girl with long stringy hair and wide, serene eyes. She moved to kneel on the far side of the animal and began to bind its legs together, all the time humming a soft tune. The old woman paid no attention.

A circle of others formed around them. A few stepped forward, muttered under their breath, and touched the animal, then stepped back. They waited patiently and silently as the old woman spoke softly into the animal's ear, and the young girl bound it tightly, front legs together, rear legs together, then strong leather thongs between the two.

When she was finished, she stood and stepped back into the surrounding circle. She raised her arms and the two men on either side of her took her hands. The circle closed in this manner, and, so slowly that it was difficult to detect, at first, they began to move in a circle.

In the center, the old woman still held the deer's head in her lap. She sang softly to it, and her fingers walked down its neck toward the chest, where her thin arrow still protruded from its side. She gripped the shaft near the base, thin, bony fingers tightening around it, the fingers of her other hand stroking the beast's muzzle. She continued like this for a few minutes longer, and then – with a swift yank – she pulled the arrow free. There was a ripple in the buck's muscles, but the paralysis held. Only in its eyes did the fear register, and there it was rampant. They rolled to white, and the woman stroked its brow. She leaned in again, spoke into the animal's ear softly, and it grew still.

She stood, and the circle broke. Dark eyed men stepped forward, caps pulled down to shield their eyes. They strung a long, sturdy pole through the leather thongs, and the others closed in at the front and rear.

"Carefully," the old woman said. "Gently. He must not be harmed. He must not touch the earth again until it is time. Do you understand?"

The men nodded. None spoke. They lifted the buck off the ground and turned, very slowly, carrying it back into the woods. The woman stepped into the trees at their side, and was gone.

Behind them, dancing across the ground where their booted feet passed, the girl followed. Her eyes were closed, and her arms were raised. Her lips moved but no sound emerged, and she danced through the trees with uncanny grace, sliding around tree trunks, and following the others into the shadows.

All that remained in the clearing was the dark, placid water, still trying to devour the shore, and the bloody arrow shaft forgotten on the soft, loamy ground.

Chapter Seven

Cletus's trailer wasn't suited for entertaining. He had a couch – somewhere. Most of the time it was covered with newspapers, books, boxes and packing material. His chair, aimed straight at the television, was the only horizontal surface he kept relatively clear. When Jasper's truck pulled up out front, the tire replaced, and the fender sporting a nice deep dent, courtesy of the Cotton Gin's ditch, Cletus stood up from his desk, looked around, blinked, and cursed.

He stumbled around the desk, cracked his knee on the corner, cursed again, and started grabbing papers and boxes and books, piling them precariously on his coffee table, the floor, and any other space not piled too high to take another layer. By the time Jasper pushed the door open, the couch was cleared.

Jasper's Pap had a twelve pack of Busch in one hand, and Earl, who stumbled along behind, had a bucket of KFC clutched like a football. Jasper looked around, saw the cleared couch and the piles of books, paper, and detritus that had been cleared off of it, grinned, and dropped onto it.

"Quick, Pap," he said, "before that crap starts fighting back and smothers us."

"Funny," Cletus said, unable to prevent the grin that split his face. "Give me one of those beers, and pay attention. We don't have much time, and we've got a lot to cover."

"You find them aliens?" Earl asked. "I got me a statement ready – for the interview."

Cletus turned and looked at the man. He started to speak, then just shook his head.

"Later, Earl. We didn't catch anyone yet, but I get the feeling that we're running out of time."

Over beer and chicken, Cletus filled the others in on what he and Bob had seen and learned in Eternity. Pap and Earl listened intently, but Jasper kept glancing longingly over at the television. Finally Cletus fell silent, watching his friend and waiting. It was a full minute after the silence began before Jasper turned and glanced up guiltily.

"What is it, Jasper?" Cletus asked. "All this talk about swamps and albinos boring you?"

"No," Jasper said. He frowned and looked back at the television. "Well, yeah. Hell, Cletus, I don't want to go mucking around in Eternity. You remember what they used to tell us about that place when we were kids. There's a race on tonight, and we got plenty of beer. Can't we just let Bob take care of this and get drunk?"

"We aren't watching any races," Cletus said. "Damn it, Jasper, you started this, so pay attention. We need to find out more about that church, and what's going on out there, and we need to do it fast. There's a man about to die, unless I miss my guess, and the FBI is probably going to try and lock up one of our neighbors for stuffing muskrats in his spare time and having a couple too many sets of antlers on his wall. We're going to stop it, and your fat ass is going to help."

Jasper tried a hurt look, but it wouldn't hold, so he grinned, grabbed another beer, and belched. "Fine. What do we do, then?"

"I wish I knew," Cletus said.

"How 'bout Nettie?" Pap asked.

"That ol' witch?" Jasper said. "What does she have to do with it?"

"She lives in the swamp near Eternity, for one thing," Cletus said, leaning back. "You might have something, Pap. You think she might help?"

"Never knowed her to be helpful, exactly," Pap said thoughtfully, "but I've heard if you show up on her doorstep with enough Bourbon, you can learn just about anything you want. You can bet one thing, she doesn't attend services at the good Reverend Dozier's church, or any other."

"I never heard of anyone named Nettie," Earl said, "But I've heard folks talk about a witch that lived out in the swamp. When I was little, my daddy used to scare us into behaving by threatening to take us out and leave us for her. I ain't in any hurry to do it to myself, now that I'm growed up. We all goin' out there?"

"Don't think that would work," Pap said. "We all show up out there, she's never going to show at all. She has a cottage not too far off the highway, just near the edge of the swamp. I don't think she lives there, but if you make enough noise getting out there, take that whiskey I mentioned, and wait on the porch, she'll show."

Cletus thought about it for a moment, then cursed under his breath.

"It's got to be me. I'm the one who saw that book in the church, and I'm the one that helped tug that – thing – out of the swamp. I'll stop by the package store in Hertford and get fifth of something on the way."

"What about the rest of us?" Jasper asked, glancing at the TV again.

"You need to get ready for a fight," Cletus said. "I don't know what's going to happen out there in Eternity, but I know they aren't going to let me walk in and stop it without a fight. You might want to get some more beer."

Cletus passed out of Hertford, glancing up at a banner slung across the road proclaiming the annual "Fall Harvest Festival" in bold letters, and turned onto Highway 17 just as the sun settled on top of the tree line. A few miles south, he turned off the main road and headed on back toward the swamp. On the seat beside him he had a fifth of Old Crow wrapped up in a plain paper bag. He felt like pulling over to the side of the road and chugging half of it, but he kept his eyes on the bumpy road. It had been a while since the county bothered to level it, and he took his time, winding around the bigger pot holes and cursing the ones he missed.

The road disappeared around a bend ahead, and he slowed, taking a deep breath. The old cottage that Pap had mentioned sat back into the trees just around that corner. Cletus had been avoiding it most of his life, starting in high school when his friends had all dared one another to pay the old place a visit late at night, and continuing through the present. He'd almost come looking for Nettie to see if he could find a story for the Weekly Globe Examiner, but at the last minute he'd decided he'd rather sell blood or work a shift at the Red Apple than knock on that door.

Now here he was.

He passed around the end of the tree line. The cottage, more of a shack, was tucked far enough back into the trees that it was visible only as a shadow among shadows. There were no lights lit, and just for a moment, Cletus considered stopping, backing up into the ditch, and heading back to town. His hands trembled, and he gripped the wheel tighter. He slowed, took a deep breath, and turned off the road onto an even bumpier track leading back under the trees.

He parked, sat, and stared at the old place for what seemed like a long time. Finally, not knowing what else to do, he opened the door of the truck, grabbed the bourbon, and stepped out of the truck. The sun had dropped the rest of the way behind the trees, and all that remained was a red, rosy glow that only seemed to emphasize the shadows. He closed the truck's door and walked slowly up a pitted sidewalk of slate rock and grit to the front porch.

There were cobwebs on the rails. Where grass grew, it was tall and ragged, but most parts of the front yard were dead, as if they couldn't support anything living too close to the frame of the old building. The floorboards of the porch were solid, but very old. They were cracked in places, warped at the ends. There were two wooden chairs placed side by side to the right of the door. Between them was a short table made from the wooden spool from phone or electric cable.

Without really knowing why, Cletus stepped up onto the porch, brushed off one of the chairs and sat down. He pulled the bottle out of its paper wrapping and placed it in the center of the table. He wished he had a flashlight, or even a candle. The moon would be up soon, but he wasn't sure he would find that silver radiance any more comforting than the shadows.

He stared off into the trees to his right, wondering what the hell he was doing. There was no one here. From the look of things, no one had been in this place in a decade, maybe longer. He closed his eyes, rubbed the bridge of his nose, started to turn and rise, and grew very still.

The light had changed. It wasn't much brighter, but it was yellow, and it flickered, sending shadows skittering in all directions. Cletus turned back to the table, and across from him, watching him in stoic silence, sat a very old woman. She was thin to the point of seeming frail. Her hair was as white as snow, but thick, falling back over her shoulders and disappearing down her back. She wore a shapeless dress of some dark material that blended with the darkness and obscured her from sight. All but her hair, and her eyes.

Cletus backed his chair up and cursed. He started to rise, but quick as a snake the old woman reached out and laid her long, slender fingers over his arm.

"I'd sit down, I was you," she said. Her voice was soft, but it carried. "Don't think I'd take myself outside that circle," she added, nodding at the plank floor.

Cletus glanced down. A rough circle had been burned into the wood. It wound around behind the table and the two chairs. He stood very still and stared at it. He hadn't been paying much attention when he walked onto the porch, and the light had been even worse, but he'd have sworn he couldn't miss something like that. He was proud of his natural instincts; he often retained details about a thing, or an event, or a face that he barely remembered noticing. None of this made the circle fade from the floor. He glanced back at the old woman, and returned to his chair.

"Been waitin' for you," she said. "Knew you'd come when it was time."

"I don't know what you're talking about," Cletus replied.

"You do, and there's no reason to deny it," she said. There was no anger or accusation in her tone. It was straightforward – almost matter-of-fact. "You going to open that bottle, or just sit there? I'm thirsty."

Glad to have something to do with his hands, Cletus reached for the bottle. His hand stopped short. There were two bottles and two glasses on the table now. The candle burned behind Nettie, showing her profile with very few details. He focused and found he couldn't tell which of the bottles was the Old Crow.

He grabbed one, twisted the top open, and poured until one of the glasses was full. He reached for the second glass, then stopped short. His fingers trembled, and he came close to dropping the bottle in his hand when he saw that the second glass was full. Nettie slid it across the table to him, then reached for the first.

"It will be harvest festival soon," she said. "You remember the harvest, don't you Cletus?"

Cletus wrapped his fingers around the glass. It was chilled, colder than it should have been, and he shivered. He glanced up and met her gaze.

"Of course I remember," he said.

"I remember too," she said. "I remember your father, Cletus. I remember your grandfather too. He used to ride in to the harvest festival in a wooden buggy pulled by two of the finest horses you've ever seen. Merle Cornelius Diggs. He was a fine figure of a man, did you know that? By the time you knew him, he was old, but I knew him in his prime."

Cletus stared across the table, trying to pierce the shadows. He knew it wasn't possible. His grandfather would have been a hundred and twenty years old if he'd sat at the table with them. The woman he was speaking with was old, there was no denying that, but she didn't seem frail, and it was very difficult to imagine she could be more than seventy.

"You couldn't have known him," he said at last. "I didn't even know him."

"I know things that would drive you crazy," she whispered. "You say you remember the festival, but I know better. You remember the watered down, hollowed-out husk of it. Like a locust skin, hanging on a fence like it was alive, and looking like it might get up and walk away – all gone. Empty."

Her voice never rose in volume, but Cletus heard her clearly.

He took a long drink from the glass in his hand. The first thing he noted was that it wasn't Old Crow. It had a taste of corn whiskey, but there was more. He had no way to judge it, but was certain that he tasted clover, and something more. He thought fleetingly about spitting it out, but it was already sliding down his throat, and the taste was intoxicating. He tried to meet the old woman's gaze and instead closed his eyes.

The breeze kicked up, and it triggered a memory. At least, it felt like a memory. He was walking across a field. The field was ripe with cotton, and he had to wind his way carefully through the plants. It seemed as if they rippled and gripped his boots. He stumbled steadily forward.

In the distance, he saw a fire. The flames licked and danced up a huge pile of wood. Figures circled that fire, but from where he walked in the field they were nothing but indistinct shadows. Beyond the fire a spread of houses lined the skyline, and he stopped, staring. Something was wrong. He scanned the horizon, and realized it was Old Mill, but not the Old Mill he knew. The houses were spread out, and too low to the ground. None of the downtown buildings stood where they should have been. He felt a cold sheen of sweat, chilled by the breeze.

When he started forward again, he caught his foot in the cotton and stumbled. He tried to right himself, hopped over a row of tall, tough green plants, caught his foot again, and sprawled. He hit the dirt hard, unable even to get his hands up in time to break his fall. He cut his cheek on a sharp cotton stalk, and his chin hit the dry, soft dirt with a soft Thunk!

He pushed himself up quickly, spitting dirt. He turned and glanced down at the foot that had caught in the row of cotton. He didn't see his Red Wings™, but instead saw that he wore some sort of shapeless leather footwear he'd never seen. His leg was smaller, but for some reason that didn't bother him as much as the boots.

He stood slowly, carefully extricating his foot and purposely keeping his eyes aimed at the ground. It was then that he noticed how quiet it was. It wasn't the quiet he'd expect in an Old Mill field, or even down at the old fishing hole by the swamp. Cletus lived in a world of sound. There was traffic in the distance, the subtle hum of neon lights, the voices and laughter of thousands of people. He heard none of it. When he stepped forward again, the air seemed thicker. He felt the sensation of walking in deep water, his questions echoing about inside his head unanswered.

The bonfire had grown taller and hotter. The ring of people dancing about its edge was an indistinct blur. They didn't turn as he approached. He walked closer, circling around the fire and giving the dancers a wide berth. He searched their faces in the shadows. As they spun past, he caught glimpses of their features. Here and there he thought he saw features he recognized, but the images were fleeting, and they moved too quickly. And they were wrong.

Like the town.

Like the idea of a huge bonfire standing on the edge of Old Mill, and the streets with too few houses, some not even standing where he remembered houses standing. And there was something else, something he recognized, but could not place. Beyond the fire, on a small mound of earth, a pole had been planted in the ground. It wasn't just a pole, though, it was a carved totem, a twisted, forked pattern of sharp tips and winding branches. The trunk rose nearly seven feet into the air, and its extremities stretched out on either side like widespread arms.

Cletus stopped and stared at it. It reached out to him over the tops of the dancers. Their motion was slowing. He glanced at them and saw they were holding hands. Their eyes were closed, and they swayed. Some of them leaned back, letting the motion of the circle and the centrifugal force prevent them from falling away from the fire. Then he noticed the woman standing alone in the center, her back to the fire. The others hadn't noticed his arrival, but she stared right at him. Through him, maybe.

The dancers slowed again. The woman raised her arms and held them out to Cletus. He met her gaze, sweat suddenly running down his forehead and winding over his cheeks. Cletus tried to step back, to turn and head for the town, or back into the field, but his legs were rooted in place as surely as if he'd grown there, and then he stepped forward. He walked straight toward the fire, and by the time he reached the dancers, they'd stopped. Cletus didn't pause as he met that ring, and the parted for him. He had an idea they'd known he was there all along – that they'd expected him, though he couldn't understand how that could be true.

He stepped through, and he saw that he knew the woman. And he didn't know the woman. Her eyes were deep green, and her corn silk blond hair glistened in the firelight. It was tied back in an intricate braid. She wore a very short, very sheer smock, tied off at the waist. She seemed to be about sixteen, or seventeen. It was hard to tell because of her eyes. They were old eyes, filled with far too much to have been gathered in a short lifetime.

She took his hands, and Cletus felt a spark of energy leap between them. He tried again to pull back, but it felt as if he were someone else. His body ignored his struggles and attempts to turn and run. As he drew closer to the woman, he pulled her against him and felt the most powerful erection of his life. He gasped out loud and gripped the girl so tightly he felt his fingers dig into her flesh. She didn't pull away. Instead, she ground her hips into him. He nearly blacked out.

The dancers were moving again. He saw them out of the corners of his eyes, but his gaze was captured by the girl, the heat emanating from her flesh, the brazen press of her flesh. The dancers circled once, twice, and then parted again. They rolled off and away from the bonfire, which he suddenly felt, blazing hot against his back, and they formed a path leading toward the strange pole he'd seen earlier. From where he stood, he saw that the branches had been carved to resemble the horns of a huge deer.

The girl turned so that they were side by side, their hips pressed tightly together. Her arm slid around the small of his back and he felt her nails bite into his flesh. They stepped forward, entering a corridor of bodies. Before the pole he now saw that a wooden table of some sort had been placed. It was covered in blankets and pillows. He shook his head to clear it, but only succeeded in fuzzing the few details that had been clear.

His arm slid around the girl's body. Someone stepped from the crowd at his right, laughing brightly. He felt hands on his shoulders; fingers ran through his hair, and then he felt an awkward weight settle over him. He tried to pull away, but every time he moved, the girl pressed herself into him in some new way, or his hand slipped and pressed a new bit of her flesh, and he lost focus. He tried to glance up, to see what they'd placed on his head, but all he caught were tangled shadows. They made no sense, but he knew they were important. He knew he should understand. He turned to the girl, just as they reached the table. She turned to meet him and melted into his arms.

"What..."

She pressed her mouth to his, lips open wide and his words were swallowed in her kiss. She fell back over the low bench, into the blankets with her silky hair spread back over the pillows and her lips parted. Cletus loomed over her. Her ankles hooked behind his thighs and pulled him forward. When he bumped the table's edge, the weight on his head overbalanced and he tumbled forward. He felt a shock and tried again to look up. This time he was able to focus. The antlers stretched up from his head and butted up against the base of the huge pole. The girl beneath him squirmed, pressing up against him.

He felt the horns gripped and tugged gently, pulled back to allow him to settle over the girl whose robes had somehow fallen away beneath her. He caught himself on his hands, but lacked the strength – or the will – to push up and away. He sank lower, and she raised her head, brushing his cheek with her lips. She reached up and grabbed his belt, loosening it with a quick tug and yanking the snap of his jeans open. His erection pulsed painfully, and he gasped as she freed it. He met her gaze for a long moment, then she arched up again. He felt her engulf him, felt her teeth grip the lobe of his ear, and heard her whispering – her voice low, husky, and hungry.

"Your daddy knew the harvest, Cletus. Your granddaddy knew more. There has always been a harvest lord. There has always been sacrifice. It makes him strong. It fires your blood."

The voice shifted with every word. It dried up. It became the sound of dust blowing over dry wood. The images faded much more slowly. The girl beneath him arched and groaned and Cletus responded, crying out, shaking his head and feeling the ponderous weight of the antlers affixed to his head tug him one way, and the back the other.

He gasped and closed his eyes. He climaxed so swiftly, and so powerfully, his thoughts flickered, died, and then flashed into a burst of light so bright that it burned. His head struck something solid, and he cursed. He pushed up and back and nearly toppled over backward. As he rose, his back struck the wall behind him and for the second time in as many moments, saw stars.

There was no sound. There was no firelight. He stood, leaning on the wall of the old shack, trying to clear his mind, and his sight. He turned, but the seat across the table was empty. Both bottles were gone. Cletus fell back into the chair. He felt a dampness in his pants he didn't want to think about. He remembered her eyes – her wrinkled, ageless skin. He looked down at the table.

In the center something had been scratched, carved quickly and crudely into the wood. He saw a rough rendition of the pole, and the antlers. He saw a church, also – identifiable by the steeple. Behind, and beneath it, there was another box. A room? It was beneath a tree, and a crude patch of flowers. Cletus stared, and his mind slipped back to Eternity. He closed his eyes and thought about the view out the back of Reverend Dozier's office.

He rose, wishing he didn't have that damp slick spot in the crotch of his jeans to think about all the way back to his trailer. He wished he could erase the image of that pole, and the heat of that fire. He wished he'd never looked into her eyes. He knew what he had to do next.

He stood shakily and staggered to his truck. Moments later he had it turned and gunned the motor, shooting down the bumpy road toward Highway 17 and Eternity.

Chapter Eight

Cletus drove back to his trailer in a daze. He was halfway to the highway before he remembered to turn on his headlights. Trees loomed on either side of the road; again and again he flinched, nearly running into the ditch each time he overreacted. He felt drained, as if he'd run ten miles, and his throat was parched and dry.

He managed to make the turn off to his trailer without an accident, and breathed a little easier. There were lights on, and he knew Jasper and the others were still there. He'd have to slip past them and change his pants – that might take some explaining – but he was glad he wouldn't be alone. He didn't know what he could tell them – didn't know if he could tell them anything – but he didn't want to be alone.

He pulled in beside Jasper's truck and stepped out, leaning heavily on his front fender until he got his bearings.

"Damn," he said.

The front door of the trailer opened and a shaft of light cut through the shadows. Jasper peered out, shading his eyes.

"Cletus? That you?" he said.

"Yeah, it's me," Cletus replied.

He stepped forward, climbed the steps to the trailer, and turned away from the light, shielding himself. He stepped around Jasper and headed straight across the room for the hallway leading to his bedroom and the bathroom beyond.

"Where you goin', Cletus?" Jasper called after him. "Jesus, what happened?"

"In a minute, Jaz," Cletus called over his shoulder. "I have to take a crap like you wouldn't believe, and my eyeballs are swimming. I'll be out in a minute."

There was no answer, but Cletus could tell from the shadow wavering just outside his bedroom door that Jasper was still there.

"What are you waitin' for Jasper?" he called out. "You thinking about coming in and holding it for me, or are you going to get me that beer?"

There was a grunt from the hall, the sound of something large crashing into the wall, and Cletus was finally alone. He grabbed another pair of jeans and some underwear and stumbled into the bathroom. He locked the door, turned on the shower, and stripped as quickly as he could manage in the small, cluttered room. Suddenly he couldn't stand the damp touch of his jeans, or the cling of his underwear. He felt limp and damp; his legs barely supported him. The only thing that kept his eyes open was the fear of the dreams that might come if he closed them. The fear that he might feel her again, pressing close to him and see the long, groping shadow of those carved horns stretching out draw him in – and down.

Cletus shook his head and stepped into the shower. The water was hot. Normally he'd turn down the temperature, but this time he welcomed the heat. He grabbed the soap and scrubbed. His arms were heavy, but he forced them into action, and before he knew it, he was grinding it into his chest, dragging it over his skin faster and faster. The water was too hot, and the coarse soap scraped and chaffed his skin, but he couldn't stop himself. The water poured down over him, and he leaned forward until he lost his balance, cracking his head into the side of the shower.

His blood roared, deafening him and he heard a loud pounding. What seemed like a long time later, he realized the pounding wasn't his heart. It was Jasper, and it sounded like he was ready to knock the door off its hinges. Cletus stood up, turned off the shower, and stared at the soap in his hand. His skin was red, raw in places. He ached over every inch of his body, but he was awake.

"Damn," he said again. Then, "Just a minute, Jasper, I'll be right out."

The pounding didn't stop immediately, but it slowed. "I'll be out in a minute," he growled. He knew it didn't sound sincere, but he didn't have any more energy to spare for it. He toweled dry quickly and gingerly, avoiding the worst of the raw areas from his bout with extreme showering, and pulled on the clean clothes. He turned the knob and opened the door slowly in case Jasper was still standing there, but the big man was seated on his bed, sipping a beer and watching the bathroom door.

"You want to tell me just what the hell that was all about?" Jasper asked. "You came crashing through here like you were on fire, locked yourself in the can and took a shower so long and hot, steam came out under the door and into the living room. Hell, Earl thought it was smoke – he was ready to call the fire department."

Feeling drained, but alert, Cletus tried a weak grin. "Let me get that beer," he said, "and I'll try to tell you. You're not going to believe it anyway, so there's no hurry."

"You find that old witch?" Jasper asked as they headed back down the hall.

Cletus nodded. "I did. Did you know the Harvest Festival was like a dried out locus shell?"

"Huh?"

Cletus stepped into the main room of his trailer, opened the fridge, grabbed a cold beer, and hit his chair hard. He didn't say a word until he'd popped the top and drained half the can.

When he looked up, he saw they were all staring at him. Earl's eyes were wide. He sipped his beer and stared like Cletus was a late-night movie. Jasper frowned and slumped back on the couch. Only Jasper's Pap watched calmly. In fact, Cletus was pretty damned sure the old bastard was smirking.

"I know where they have him," Cletus said at last. "I took her the whiskey, like you said, Pap, but she drugged me. I saw some crazy shit – and I'd be lying if I said I was okay, but I got what I went there for. At least, I think I did."

"What?" Earl asked. "She give you a vision?"

"You might say that," Cletus replied, taking another long swallow of beer. "Thing that matters is, she drew me a picture of that church out in Eternity. Remember I told you there was a sort of weird little garden out back by that tree? Seems there might be something there after all – an old root cellar, or something worse. I'm betting that guy who was abducted is down there, and I'm betting he won't be okay for long. The Harvest Festival is only a few days from now."

"What the hell does the festival have to do with anything?"

Jasper asked. He belched, stared at the empty can in his hand, and lurched to his feet to get another.

"Toss me one," Cletus said. Then he continued.

"It isn't about funnel cake and bratwurst. At least, it wasn't always about that. That woman – Nettie – said she knew my dad. She said she knew my granpa too. What I saw – what she made me see, somehow – was old. I don't know how, but I swear she showed me Old Mill like it was a hundred years ago. Most of the houses weren't there, and there was a bonfire – a big one. It was outside town."

"You see that pole?" Pap cut in. The old man sipped his beer and met Cletus' gaze, but his hand shook.

Cletus fell silent and stared, then nodded. "I did. Damn thing looked like a telephone pole with antlers. I've never seen anything like it."

"Yes you have," Pap said softly. "You've seen it a hundred times, maybe more. You too, Jasper."

Cletus stared. Jasper looked like he was about to say something about his father's mental faculties, but before he could get a sound out, Pap went on.

"You've been down to the lodge, Cletus. How many times? Your daddy brought you there when you were no taller than a beer cooler. You telling me you never looked around that place? You never hid in the corners, or explored?"

"Sure I did," Cletus said, irritated at being interrupted. "So what?"

"You never hid up by the fireplace? Never looked up to the left?"

Cletus closed his eyes and tried to picture what Pap was talking about. He'd never joined the lodge – though his father had wanted him to. He'd been too busy, and it seemed like nothing more than a bunch of old guys convinced the border of Old Mill was the edge of the world. It was depressing, and he figured he'd save his time there for when he was pulling his pants up to the middle of his chest and farting in public.

The fireplace Pap was talking about was one of the most remarkable things about the lodge. It was huge, the mantle carved of stone with animals in relief below the ledge. The bricks were very old, and Cletus remembered they were scorched and black.

He tried to remember the corners of the room to either side, and suddenly his face paled. He nearly dropped the beer Jasper handed him.

Pap nodded as he saw understanding dawning in Cletus' eyes.

"Yep," the old man said. "That's it. That damned pole is set into the corner of the building. They put it there to keep them from carrying it out to that field. They tried to come in and take it back, and our folks had to threaten to burn it – building and all. There's still some back toward the swamp who come down and stand outside the Lodge come Harvest. They stand across the street, and they stare. They blame us for what's happened to the cotton – the Mill closing, the crop being shipped overseas, the way the fields are drained to the point where even chemicals and topsoil and fertilizer can't bring it back. Sometimes, when I see their eyes...I wonder if they aren't right."

"You remember," Cletus said softly. "You know what I saw – what they were doing. That table – and the woman. Was it Nettie?"

"It hasn't always been her, not exactly," Pap said. He was staring at a point on the wall somewhere above Cletus as if he saw through to some other place, or time. "There were always two – an old woman, and a young girl. The girl was the harvest queen."

Pap grew silent then, and they all waited while he gathered his thoughts. It was obvious that some doorway, or window, into his past had been pried open. Cletus handed the old man another beer, and sat back.

"Your pa was supposed to be a harvest lord, Cletus. That was the year they locked away that damnable pole. Your grandpa was Harvest Lord before him, and he was never the same after. I was just a boy, you know...my memory is good, but that was a very long time ago.

"I remember the old woman, and I'd swear they called her Nettie, but I remember the girl too. She was a looker – thin and dressed in a sheer, cotton dress. In those times women didn't dress that way – not ever – but come harvest, the blinders went on and nobody noticed. Nobody said a thing."

"What was the Harvest Lord?" Cletus asked. He was afraid he already knew the answer, but he had to ask.

"You said you saw that table – that bed," Pap said softly. "Your grandpa Merle, he walked down that line, and that girl went with him. He didn't have the luxury you did of waking up. Can't say I remember how it ended – not exactly – but I remember this. It wasn't a week later I saw that girl, and she was carryin' a child. Not showing a little, like you'd think might be possible, but ready to pop. The old woman – I never saw her again. The girl grew up and when we took that damned pole, she moved out of town. Out off 17. She had a daughter."

"Nettie," Cletus whispered.

Pap nodded. "I think so. Leastways I can't figure any other way it could be. That shack where you were sitting on the porch? That's where they moved. For a long time, no one heard anything from them. Sometimes the women would go there, if they were sickly, or if there was something they needed. Sometimes even the older men would slip off to that cabin when the sun was down, bottles of whiskey in hand and things on their minds best left to the imagination – or forgotten altogether. She never came back to the Harvest Festival when they started holding it again. I never went either. It seemed empty somehow." Pap took another swig of beer and shook his head. Then he actually chuckled.

"What's so damned funny?" Jasper asked. He looked confused, and a little too drunk to piece together all he'd just heard from his best friend and his father.

"Just thinking," Pap said. "What Cletus said – what Nettie said – about a locust skin. It's exactly right."

"Locusts swarm the fields and eat everything in sight," Cletus cut in. "They raze the crops, leave people hungry, and if you walk out into them at the wrong time, they'll kill you."

Pap nodded slowly. "I know. I think maybe I'll get on over to the lodge and make sure things are locked up and secure. I haven't seen anyone standing down there yet this year, but damned if I don't get the idea they might. Maybe I'll take me some lighter fluid and matches, while I'm thinking about it – just in case."

"That might not be a bad idea," Cletus said. "As a backup. We've got us some work to do. Jasper, we have to get some things together. Earl? I'm going to ask you to do me a big favor. I want you to hightail it over to the Sheriff's office and get Bob."

They all rose, and Earl stared dubiously at the beer can in his hand. Cletus followed the big man's gaze and frowned.

"Ditch that," he said. "Get on the phone, call Bob, and tell him to get his ass over here. Tell him Cletus says he has a date with Eternity, and he'd better not be late."

"What about the Troopers," Jasper cut in. "Shouldn't we call them off their taxidermist hunt?"

"How you going to explain it to them, Jasper? You going to tell them it can't be a taxidermist because your ol' buddy Cletus, the fella out by the swamp who's a preacher, a reporter, a common law lawyer and likes rasslin' had a drunken vision on the swamp witch's porch, and he figures they should give up what they're thinking and head out to Eternity to raid the garden behind the church instead?"

Jasper stared at him, then guzzled the last of his beer. "You ain't gotta be a smartass, Cletus. And while you're at it, maybe you ought to think about the fact that you just described exactly what we're about to do."

"Yeah, Jaz," Cletus grinned, "but we're just a bunch of rednecked jackasses, so who will be surprised?"

He turned toward the door, and Earl headed for the phone, and Pap was already on his way out the door. Jasper tossed his empty at the trash can, missed, belched, and followed Cletus out into the night.

Chapter Nine

By the time Cletus and Jasper returned to the trailer, Bob's Land Rover was parked outside. Jasper's truck was still missing, and Cletus hoped that Pap was going to be okay. In the back of Cletus' truck several bundles were tucked up near the cab and covered with a blue tarp. The two of them climbed out and headed into the trailer.

They found Bob and Earl in front of the TV. On the screen, colorful cars roared in endless circles. Both men looked up – Bob with a frown, and Earl looking like he was going on his first Boy Scout hike.

"This better be good, Cletus," Bob said. "I'm on tonight – they're screaming for me to be out on 17 covering an accident, and I told them I was following something more important. Please tell me I'm following something more important."

Cletus started to answer, but Bob turned and nodded at Earl.

"Earl here tells me we're either going out to hunt aliens, or chasing off to Eternity after a swamp witch. I think when this is all over and done we should have us a talk about recruiting."

"Earl is the only witness to the abduction," Cletus said. "We may owe it to his family, his future wife and children, and the entire state of North Carolina to make sure he understands, before this is over, that there were no aliens in pickup trucks at the Gin the other night."

Bob shook his head and held his tongue.

Cletus quickly filled him in on his evening, including only the pertinent facts. He saw no reason to linger on the bonfire, or the girl in his dream. He didn't think it was the appropriate time to toss time-traveling visions into the mix if he wanted Bob's help.

"You know they're out there, Bob," Cletus said at last. "There was a hell of a lot Dozier didn't tell us when we were at that church, and I told you what I saw out back."

"I remember," Bob said. "You saw a tree and an oddly placed flower bed. The man was standing beside it."

"There's a cellar," Cletus said. "That's what Nettie was telling us, and I've got a feeling that if we don't get out there and open it up, we're going to have another floating deer man on the edge of the swamp, or worse. Maybe this time he won't die."

Bob stared at Cletus, and his eyes went flat.

"That ain't possible, Cletus, and I won't listen to it. You want me to believe there's a couple of albino geniuses carving a sailor up out in the swamp, I'm up for that. Maybe there is, maybe there isn't. You want me to believe some old witch traded you valuable information for a bottle of whiskey – that's good investigating, though I doubt the county would authorize me the whiskey. You tell me some guy with a deer's head is going to romp through the swamp, and that's where it ends. I'll pack up, head back to the office, and watch the rest of the race. We straight?"

Cletus stared at him for a moment longer, and then nodded. "We are. And if we do see something that shouldn't be moving, we'll make sure it stops."

Bob didn't answer, but Cletus knew they were on the same channel.

"Where you keep the shells?" Jasper called out from across the trailer.

Everyone in the room spun and stared. Jasper had a ten gauge shotgun under his arm, the barrels pointed slightly up at an angle over their heads. Cletus and Bob backed in opposite directions, cursing.

"Put that damned thing down, Jasper," Cletus growled. He stumbled across the room, but Jasper pulled the gun back just before he could get his hands on it.

"No way, Cletus," he said. "If we're going out to that church, I'm not going unarmed. I know you're packing, and Bob there has a gun rack full outside, and one on his belt. What was your plan – me and Earl as bait while you shot from behind the trees?"

Cletus stepped back. Jasper was right, and he knew it. None of them knew how dangerous this night might get. He turned to Earl.

"You know how to work a .45?" he asked. "I've got an old Navy issue in the dresser beside my bead."

"I can shoot," Earl said. He puffed up his chest and grinned like a schoolboy.

Bob turned away, shook his head again, and made an issue of looking through the papers on Cletus' desk. Cletus stepped out of the room and down the hall in back, returning with the pistol and handing it to Earl butt first.

"It's loaded," he said. "Safety is on. Don't take it off until we are OUT of the truck."

"Don't shoot anyone unless we're about to die," Bob growled at all of them. "Seriously, Cletus, I can see a hundred ways this can go bad, and not a one that makes it right. I can't deputize any of you without calling in and making reports and getting backup that they won't authorize in the first place, but that doesn't change the fact that I'm responsible for this half-ring circus. I don't want any of you getting hurt. We're going in, getting some answers out of Reverend Dozier, or whoever we find out there, and taking a look around that flower bed. If we find nothing, we're out of there, and that's the end of it."

"What if them aliens come after us?" Earl asked.

Bob turned to the door in disgust and pushed through, heading into the night. The door swung shut behind him with a clatter.

Cletus took a deep breath, patted Earl on the back, and followed Bob.

"Lock the door behind us, Jasper," he called. "No telling when we'll be back, and I don't need anyone digging through my stuff."

Jasper snorted.

"They'd have to bring a big shovel to find anything worth takin'" he said.

Cletus ignored him, and Jasper locked the door. Once outside, Bob was all business. He took Earl in the Land Rover, and Jasper climbed in beside Cletus. Cletus backed up so the two vehicles were side by side, and they rolled down their windows.

"You follow us in," Bob said. "I've got better traction, and if they see us coming, I want them to see an official vehicle."

Cletus nodded. Bob turned to Earl, grabbed his shirt and dragged him close.

"You say another goddamn word about aliens, and I'll kick your ass out on the road to walk home from the swamp. We clear?"

Earl gulped, but had the sense to nod. He started to say something, then bit it off. Cletus smiled.

Bob backed up quickly, spun and started down Cletus' drive toward the road and the highway beyond. Cletus took a quick half-circle and followed. The moon was full and high in the sky, illuminating the fields around them like a pale sun.

Jasper leaned down, grabbed something off the floor, then sat back up. Cletus glanced over just in time to watch the pop top on a Budweiser snap and fizz. He started to say something, and then held out his hand. Jasper grinned, handed over the beer and reached for another.

"Ooh fuckin' Rah," Cletus said, lifting his can just high enough it didn't show over the windshield in salute.

They drove in silence, and Cletus was eerily reminded of his earlier trip with Bob. Once they'd turned off of the main roads everything changed. It was like driving into the past, and it was harder and harder to remember even the semi-civilization that was his trailer in the face of the rich scent of rotted vegetation, the rolling hills and trees, and the hypnotic rise and fall of headlights as the two vehicles rumbled down the poorly maintained road.

When they neared the last corner that turned into the main road into Eternity, it was immediately obvious that things had changed. The glow of lights hung like a shimmering halo over the trees. As dead and empty as the town had seemed, it was now alive. It should have seemed more cheerful – at least that's what Cletus told himself – but it was impossible to push aside the sensation of standing too close to a buzzing beehive. The last thing he wanted to do was poke that place with a sharp stick.

Bob slowed before he reached the corner, and Cletus pulled in behind him. He got out and walked up toward the Land Rover. He only noticed he was still carrying the beer can just in time to toss it into the trees beside the road as he stepped up beside Bob's window. Bob stared pointedly at the point where the can had flashed out of sight, shook his head, and let it go.

"There's something going on up there, Cletus,"

"I know," Cletus said. "I can see the glow from the lights. You think they're just having a late night service?"

"I'm not sure I'd want to be there, even if that's the case," Bob answered. "I just can't help thinking that if there's something twisted going on in or around that church, all of them are in on it. How would he hide it from them? We don't have enough manpower to take on the whole congregation."

Cletus glanced across Bob to where Earl sat.

'I'm not sure we have enough manpower to take on the empty church. What you want to do, Bob?"

The answer was cut off by the roar of an engine, closely followed by several more. Cletus stared at Bob, then turned and ran for his truck. Bob pulled ahead, and just as Cletus swung in behind the wheel again, he saw the Land Rover turn right, instead of left. He vaguely recalled that there was a rough trail leading off the main road, and he hoped that Bob had found it and wasn't going four-wheeling and leaving Cletus to follow on two.

Moments later he was bouncing down a narrow, single lane pair of ruts no one could charitably call a road, and clinging to the wheel grimly to keep the truck from bouncing off into the trees. Then Bob's lights went out, and Cletus killed his engine. He turned just enough to see a line of headlights approaching from the rear. He held his breath until the first swung to the right and disappeared down the road where he'd just been parked.

"Holy shit, Cletus," Jasper said, finding his voice. "What the hell is goin' on?"

"Damned if I know," Cletus muttered. He heard the snap of another beer opening and closed his eyes, waiting for the wash of headlights across his eyelids to stop and tell him everyone who was leaving the church had gone.

"Where are they going, Cletus," Jasper asked.

Cletus was about to snap at his friend, when something clicked in his mind.

"Damn it," he said. He stepped out of his truck and ran ahead to where Bob had pulled up against the trees.

"They're headed to Old Mill," he said. "Bob, I think they're after that damned horned pole at the lodge. Can you raise dispatch on your radio?"

Bob looked unconvinced, but he took Cletus seriously enough to believe there was danger. He grabbed the microphone and keyed it.

"Four-one to base. Come in base."

There was a squawk, and a quick burst of static, then silence.

"Damn it," Bob said. He tried again, but there was no answer.

"Hey," Earl said.

"Not now, Earl," Cletus snapped. "We have a serious problem here. You think if we drove back down the road a ways we could get through?" he asked Bob, who was fiddling with dials on the radio.

"Hey!" Earl said, raising his voice.

This time Bob spun on him, but before he could say a word, Earl thrust something into his face, and he bit his lip. Earl was holding a small cell phone, the type you buy at the 7-11 and pay for ahead of time. The lights were lit on the small dial, and even from where he stood, Cletus could see there were two signal bars.

"Use this," Earl said.

Bob stared as Cletus leaned over, snatched the phone from Earl, and started to dial. The glowing dial of his radio glimmered up at him, and he frowned.

"Just how in hell," he said.

Cletus held up his hand.

"Jim?" he asked. There was a short silence, and then Cletus cut off whatever it was that Jim had to say. "I don't have time for that now, Jim. I know I owe you, and I'll pay, but you've got to listen. This is important – not like Smackdown is on and we're out of beer important, but the real deal. You kapish?"

Another short silence, and Cletus nodded.

"Good. Get as many guys as you can and get over to the Lodge in Old Mill. Jasper's Pap is there, and I think he's in trouble. There's a whole convoy of the friends of Jesus of Eternity on their way in there, and I think they intend to burn the place down. See if you boys can't stop them. You can tell everyone these are the bastards that have the troopers running around hassling anyone who ever stuffed a deer, if that helps.

"No, I haven't been drinking. You going to do this, or do you want to talk to Bob. Yes….Sheriff Bob. He's right here with me. No…I'm not telling him that." This time Cletus did grin. "Tell you what, if we make it back to town in one piece, I'll let you tell him yourself."

Cletus disconnected the line and tossed the phone back to Earl.

"No wonder we can't get the drug dealers off the streets," Bob muttered. "They have all the high-tech equipment."

"I ain't no..." Earl started to protest. Bob held up a hand to silence him.

"Forget it," he said. "Let's get this over with before they come back."

Cletus returned to his truck and started the engine. It took a bit longer to back out onto the main road, but eventually he managed it. He backed far enough down the road that Bob could get out and followed the Land Rover on around the corner into Eternity.

There were lights on in the church, but not as many as there had been before. The door was closed, and there was a single vehicle in the parking lot. It was a black pickup truck. Bob pulled in beside it, and Cletus pulled in beside Bob.

Earl was out of the Land Rover before it came to a full stop, and as Cletus stepped out onto the parking lot he heard the big man speaking excitedly, and Bob trying to calm him down.

"That's it!" Earl whispered so loudly he might as well have shouted. "That's the truck they took him in. That's the truck that had the alie...albinos."

Cletus stared at it for a moment, and Jasper stepped up behind him.

"I think he's right, Cletus. I only saw it for a minute, but it was up pretty damned close, you know?"

Cletus nodded and turned to Bob, who already had the flap over his gun unsnapped.

"Cletus, you and me are going around back to check out that flowerbed. Jasper, you take Earl here, and get the good reverend's attention. Tell him you got drunk and turned the wrong way. You've had enough beer that he'll believe you."

"What if he don't?" Earl asked. "I ain't had as much to drink as Jasper."

"Ask him about the aliens," Cletus suggested, grinning. "Tell him you saw a saucer drop down out in the swamp near here, and you drove out to see if you could find it."

"Whatever you do," Bob said, "Don't let him come out back. Not until you see us. We'll either know what the hell is going on, or we'll know nothing is going on that's any of our business."

Jasper didn't look convinced. Cletus slapped him on the back.

"It's been long enough since you went to church, Jaz," he said.

"I come to your trailer all the time," Jasper said pointedly. "You ARE ordained."

Bob snorted, turned, and started around the side of the church. Cletus glanced a last time at the black pickup truck, then followed. Jasper and Earl crunched up the gravel walk toward the church. The silence surrounding them was as deep as a tar pit and twice as sticky.

Chapter Ten

Bob rounded the corner of the church with his gun drawn, and Cletus moved up close behind him. He wished there had still been some people milling about, or that there was light or sound from somewhere other than the church. It was like they'd stepped through the screen into some weird Twilight Zone adventure. There were a couple of lights on poles that lit the parking lot, and they hummed so loudly Cletus thought he could hear the electricity running through the wires. The sensation of being watched was so strong he couldn't help jerking his head around and looking over his shoulder every few seconds. There was nothing to see.

Bob seemed jumpy as well, but he was trained to this sort of work, and he moved steadily forward. He had his gun trained forward into the shadows, and he remained focused, trusting Cletus to watch his back. They reached the back corner of the building without incident, and then Bob did look back. He motioned Cletus forward so he could whisper.

"I'm going to cross over to that tree a quick as I can. You follow, but not 'til I'm over there, and we're sure no one sets off an alarm. If they see me, don't show yourself until you have to. We may need to get the jump on them, and I don't want to trust that to Jasper and Earl."

Before Cletus could answer, Bob stepped away from the building and started across the rear lawn of the church. He stayed in a crouch, but moved quickly and quietly. Cletus tensed, but there was no outcry. There was no flash of light to indicate doors or windows opening. There was no change in the deep quiet, or the hum of the lights overhead.

Bob reached the tree, disappeared for a second into its shadow, and then waved for Cletus to join him. With a last glance over his shoulder, that's exactly what he did. He tried to emulate Bob's crouching run, but his legs complained, and with a shrug he stood up straight and ran. Moments later Bob pulled him down into the shadows, and the two of them hunkered down in silence.

From where they squatted, they could see the rear window and door of the church. There was a light on in Reverend Dozier's office, but for the moment no silhouettes moved beyond it. Cletus hoped that meant Jasper and Earl had the good Reverend's attention in the church proper. All alternatives were bad.

"Keep an eye on the door," Bob hissed.

Cletus nodded, and Bob turned, using his free hand to root around in the leaves and flowers. There was plenty of light in the yard, but there under the tree they were in shadow, and most of the ground looked the same. Cletus wanted to be looking too. Squatting in the dark was last on his current list of favorite things, but he knew Bob was right. They couldn't afford not to keep a careful watch on the church. If Dozier came up behind them and caught them rooting around, there was no telling what he might do – or who he might have available to call for backup.

Bob let out a quick grunt of surprise, and Cletus heard him scrabbling for footing.

"Damn," Bob said.

Cletus turned. Bob was seated in the dirt, staring at the metal handle in his hand, and the wooden door that had risen from the leaves and brush when he pulled. He held onto it and scrambled back to his feet. There was a dim glow of light beyond the door, somewhere beneath them. They waited – but there was no sound. Whoever or whatever was down there had apparently not heard them.

Cletus glanced back at the church. The window still glowed like a big, empty eye, glaring out at them. No sigh of Dozier, or anyone else.

"You ready for this?" Bob asked.

"Nope," Cletus replied.

Bob grinned, pulled the door the rest of the way open and lowered it to the ground. He worked his way slowly around it and took a step down. Cletus took a deep breath, and followed. By the time he reached the steps, Bob was out of sight except for a dark silhouette moving down into a very dimly lit interior. Cletus wondered briefly if he should stop and pull the door closed behind them, but decided against it. They might need to get back out of there quickly, and the last thing he needed was to run head-first into a wooden door.

The second he started down the stairs, the stench hit him, and he nearly retched. It was thick, and viscous. Antiseptic, chemical vapors mixed with something more familiar. He couldn't trace the memory that itched at his brain, but he knew that scent, and it repelled him. Bob was already out of sight, and he knew he had to keep going, but every instinct he had told him it was a bad idea.

"Story of my life," he muttered. He took the remaining steps more quickly, pulling his .45 as he went. He hadn't heard Bob cry out, but that didn't mean there wasn't trouble. No sense walking into it without protection, for what it was worth. His eyes watered from the acrid fumes, and he wondered if the air below was even breathable, but it had been his idea to come here and investigate, and he couldn't back out now that Bob was in the middle of it, whatever "it" was.

As he reached the bottom step, he saw that a doorway opened on the right. The light beyond that corner was brighter. Whoever had designed the stairs and the cellar had clearly taken into account blocking the light from below from visibility above. Such forethought was a bad sign. Cletus rounded the corner, and stopped dead in his tracks. Directly ahead of him, Bob was stopped as well, his gun arm slack at his side.

Cletus barely noticed. He stared past Bob at a stainless steel table against the far wall of the cellar.

It was like a bad "B" movie nightmare. The surface of the table, which was about four foot square, was nearly covered by a large, round, glass tank. The tank was made of clear glass, or Plexiglas, and it was filled nearly to the brim with some sort of greenish fluid. Tubes and wires snaked over the top and into the liquid, which bubbled and frothed. Cletus hardly noticed.

In the center of the tank, staring at him with wild eyes rolled nearly to whites in its head, the head of a white-tail buck stared sightlessly back at him. There was no way the thing could be alive, but he saw its ears twitch. The nostrils flared, and Cletus was sure he saw movement under its skin, as if something were crawling up and down its throat.

"Jesus H. Freaking Christ," Bob whispered.

Cletus wanted to respond, but he couldn't find a single phrase in all his colorful cursing lexicon to cover it. Something splashed in the tank, and he felt as if his heart had exploded and all the blood, ice cold, had tried to seep out through his skin. It just wasn't possible – not that it existed, or that he could possibly wrap his mind around it. He saw the thing's shadow on the wall behind it, dark antlers stretching up toward the ceiling and out of sight.

"Amazing, isn't he?"

The voice was very close. It had no volume, and yet it snapped through the silent horror in the room like a whip. Cletus spun, but it was too late. As he turned, he heard the hiss of something being sprayed. He tasted something sickly sweet and his eyelids were instantly heavy. He tried to turn and lift his gun hand, but it was too heavy. He spun, and he couldn't stop the momentum. It carried him in a staggering circle.

Someone stood beside him, and he reached out, but the small, very pale man stepped back almost casually. Cletus rolled past him and fell. Behind him he heard Bob grunt, and knew it was too late for his friend, as well. The man who'd sprayed him with – what? He was one of the twins. There were two. The room spun and Cletus tried, and failed, to focus his eyes. Before he went out completely, he heard a heavy thud, and he knew Bob was down too.

When he came to, the first thing Cletus noticed was the smell. He couldn't place it, and he shook his head slowly, which was a mistake. He had a pounding headache that threatened to drop him back into darkness, or make him puke. He tried to move and found he was seated in a straight backed chair. His hands were bound behind him – it felt like duct tape. He closed his eyes, counted to ten, and opened them again. This time the room came to life, and he nearly tipped the chair over backward in shock and disgust, pushing back with both legs. Someone stood behind him, and they easily prevented him from moving.

Bob was tied in a chair beside him, already awake. The sheriff's eyes were glued to the table across the room and the strange tank.

A small man stood beside him, young, and pale, white-blond hair unkempt and small, pink eyes blinking slowly. He, too, watched the tank, and Cletus followed their gaze. After a moment, he realized the guy was talking.

"He truly is magnificent, isn't he? Nothing like this has ever been attempted before."

"We attempted it, of course," a second voice chimed in from behind Cletus and to the left. "We attempted it just last week, with some success."

"But never before, brother, never before," the first man said, nodding and smiling, as if they were discussing a chess move over cocktails.

In the tank, the severed deer's head was showing more animation than it had when Cletus first saw it. He didn't know if all the lights and commotion had disturbed it, or if whatever they were doing to it in that tank had just progressed further, but the thing glared at them. The muscles of its neck rippled, and it lowered its antlers slightly, as if readying to charge. This motion was arrested by what appeared to be a network of bungee cords attaching it to the wall.

"Now now," the voice behind Cletus said softly. "Calm down. We mustn't damage ourself before the procedure is complete. Oh now, too much to do – too many people waiting on you."

"The Reverend is waiting," the first man added. "He is anxious to meet you, and the witch."

"She's not a witch," the second voice cut in. "Not exactly. There is an aspect of old world religious about her, but she is clearly attuned with the earth – the swamp to be exact."

"Yes, yes, but..."

That was all Cletus could take. He cleared his throat and put on the angriest scowl he could muster through the pounding in his head. His lips felt like they'd been glued together, and his words were garbled.

"I don't know who the hell you two are," he said, "or what that thing over there is supposed to be – though I have a pretty good idea on that. You boys made a mistake here, though. You've assaulted and abducted a man of the law."

"We didn't make a mistake," the first man said.

"Oh, no, that would be unlikely," the second cut in.

"Statistically," the first said, "we are correct about ninety-nine point two percent of the time. There are aspects of our training we are still fleshing out, but to be outright incorrect is…"

Bob was paying little or no attention to any of it. His gaze was glued to the tank, and his mouth hung open in a way Cletus didn't care for. It reminded him too much of the way Bob had stood over the body back at the swamp. Cletus didn't know how they were going to get out of this one, but he knew he had to get Bob back, and quickly.

"Yeah, just for the hell of it, why don't you boys tell us what you've made for the science fair?"

The voice behind Cletus belonged to another short, pale young man, so identical to the first that when he stepped around into view, it was like they were images facing one another in a mirror. Coupled with the way they finished each other's sentences, and the fact he could now see they moved like they were ganged together with gears and levers, the whole scene dropped fast towards The Twilight Zone without a parachute.

"He's our lifework," the first said.

"Actually, he really is our life, isn't he?" the second replied.

"You boys have names?" Cletus growled? "And while you're at it, you think you could finish one sentence at a time – or maybe tag each other when you change back and forth?"

Both brothers turned and stared at him. They didn't look angry. He could almost hear gears whirring as they processed what he'd said and tried to apply it to the situation through their own logic. Finally, the first brother said.

"I'm Weston," he said.

"I'm David," his brother chimed in. They walked toward Cletus, crossing as they passed around Bob's chair, and Cletus felt a moment of vertigo. He couldn't tell which was which. As they came to a stop directly in front of him, leaned in and peered at him as if he were in a giant Petri dish of his own, he decided it didn't matter. Until he figured out a better plan, he needed to keep them talking.

"Your buddy over the have a name too?" he asked.

They stopped, momentarily confused. Then Weston smiled – at least he thought it was Weston.

"It's an interesting question," he answered. "He has no name, but then, he isn't whole yet."

"The other has a name, I believe," David said helpfully. "Perhaps there will be enough left of him to remember?"

"Familial memory in the genetic code?" Weston asked.

"Residual synapses from the electro-chemical system they call a soul?" David pondered.

"Maybe one of you could tell me why that head isn't dead," Cletus said, trying to keep their attention.

Weston's head swiveled back and he smiled at Cletus.

"Of course we can tell you. We are responsible."

"A foolishly worded question," David agreed. "However, it is possible it's based on a genuine curiosity about our work."

Cletus nodded, not trusting his mouth in the area of self-preservation.

"It's simple, really," Weston said.

"Elementary," David added.

"The microbes we created, tiny nano-doctors, really, are reconfiguring his – its – molecular structure. It's like a computer."

"You can reprogram a computer to use a new operating system," David said.

"You can interface with the old hardware, as well," Weston continued.

"You're turning it into something else?" Bob blurted.

Cletus glanced over and saw that Bob's face, while pale and beaded with sweat, was animated again. For what it was worth, Bob was back in the game.

"More precisely," David answered. "We already have changed it into something else. It could exist as it is for a very long time, feeding off the fluids we provide and unable to release itself from the tank."

"Not as elegant as the whole," Weston added.

"Incomplete," David agreed. "We would never leave a work in such a state, but it is already remarkable."

"Unique," Weston suggested.

"Twisted," Bob muttered.

Both twins grinned at this, and Cletus wondered just what they really thought about the – thing – that they'd created. He wondered if they had a concept of God, other than an endless, two-voiced, single-minded conversation about cosmic entities. In the back of his mind, Cletus heard a muffled sound behind him.

Not sure if that sound was help, or just the Reverend coming to check up on his handiwork, he had to think quickly.

"How does it attach?" he blurted. "To the man? How do you make that – thing – bond with the body? Aren't transplants tricky, even with two humans?"

"Much better!" Weston beamed. If he'd heard the sound, he did not let on, and his face had taken on more emotion than Cletus had seen since they'd stepped from the shadows.

"Excellent," David agreed. "That is the point, isn't it?"

"What point?" Bob asked. He didn't seem to have heard the sound either, and Cletus started to wonder if it had all been in his mind, but he kept on.

"The subject must be fresh," Weston said.

"Not like the head," David agreed. "There must be as little disruption as possible in the central nervous system, so the microbes can assimilate the entirety of the logic involved."

"Very complex," Weston explained. "The human mind and body are much more difficult to control than, say, a portable computer. You can't reboot."

"No good backup system," David pointed out. "You get one shot."

Before Cletus could respond, there was a slamming sound from above. Muffled curses filled the air, and a huge clatter rose from the stairs. The two brothers turned, not moving from where they'd been standing. Weston blinked. David raised an eyebrow and frowned.

Jasper crashed into the wall at the base of the stairs, hit the wall hard, and rolled into the room, sprawled across the floor. He reached feebly for the rifle he'd held, but it was just out of his reach, and Weston was already moving toward it. He would have gotten the weapon from Jasper easily, if, at that moment, Earl hadn't roared around the corner, the shotgun at chest level, screaming like a banshee.

"Git 'er Done!"

David stepped back. Earl saw the deer's head, snout lifted to the air and eyes rolling. He stopped, just for a second. His jaw dropped, and then – without hesitation, he raised the gun and pulled the trigger.

The report of the shotgun in that tiny chamber was deafening. Cletus felt the buckshot whip past his ear and ruffle his hair, and he saw the deer's head explode in a spray of green fluid, fur, and flesh. Earl followed the shot into the room, bringing the butt of the gun against David's head in a solid crack of sound that toppled the man. He leveled the gun at Weston, who simply backed against the wall and stared.

Jasper rose slowly, rubbing his shoulder.

"Get us out of here," Cletus growled. "Jesus, Earl, you got that microbe crap all over everything."

"Technically," Weston commented, as if watching the entire thing from a balcony seat, "there is no crap. Excrement would not occur until the bodies were joined…"

Earl turned and cracked Weston hard in the head, shutting him up.

As Jasper untied Cletus, Earl stepped up and did the same for Bob.

"You find the guy?" Earl asked.

"No," Cletus said, "but there's a back room. He's probably in there."

"Cletus, you check it out," Bob said, standing and rubbing his wrists. "Take Earl with you. Jasper and I will secure these boys. Where's the reverend?"

"Tied up in his office," Jasper said. "Earl shot him in the foot."

Bob blinked. He started to say something, and the color returned very suddenly to his face, but then he held up a hand. "I don't even want to know," he said. "Let's get them out of here and into the Land Rover. We'll see what we can do about the good Reverend's foot on the way."

Cletus didn't wait to watch the brothers exit from their lab. He had bits and pieces of greenish deer meat and droplets of green chemical all over him, and he was nearly certain he felt his skin crawling. He needed to get this over with and get out of that pit – into some light and near to some water. Hell, he thought he might dive head first into the swamp if he needed to kill the double-D Goddamned MICROBES before they infected his system.

He pushed open the curtain leading deeper into the cellar, and Earl followed. There was a dim light in the next room, and almost immediately he made out a prone figure, bound, gagged, and lying on a hard cot in the corner. From where he stood, he saw the glint of the man's eyes, and knew they weren't too late. He rushed to the cot, knelt down, and quickly began unbinding the man's hands. Next he pulled off the tape they'd used to gag him, garnering a sharp gasp of pain as the sticky binding tore at the man's mustache and skin.

"Thank God." Cletus helped the man to his feet, and Earl turned, watching the doorway behind him as if he still thought the deer in the next room might re-assemble and come in after them.

"Let's get you out of here, friend," Cletus said, helping the man to his feet. He was stiff from lying in one position for too long, and Cletus figured the guy must have to piss like a racehorse, but they needed to get into the fresh air. They hurried through the outer lab and up the stairs. Above them, the moon was full and bright, and they could see the lights on in the Reverend's office.

"Let's get in there," Cletus said. "I've got to get this crap off of me, and we have to figure out what to do. The rest of the Good Reverend's folks aren't going to take this too well, and I don't want to be here when they return."

They entered the back of the church, and Cletus spared Reverend Dozier only a quick glance. He saw the man was bound to his own office chair, and that his face was pale and awash in pain. His shoe has been removed, and Cletus saw that Bob had applied bandages as best he could. The Reverend's prisoner, whose name they still hadn't even asked, dropped heavily into a chair across the desk from Dozier, who began looking, if anything, even more uncomfortable.

Jasper looked up as Cletus made a beeline for the bathroom.

"You think Pap is okay, Cletus?" Jasper asked. "They've been gone a long time."

"We'll go after them, Jasper," Cletus said. "This isn't finished by far."

"You got that right," Bob piped in. He stepped out of the main room of the church and back into the hall outside the office. "I still can't get anyone on the radio, but I think we'd better high-tail it back to Old Mill and see what's going on. I can't get the image of that old carved tree out of my head, now that you put it there, Cletus. I don't know how, but I know that's what they're after, and something tells me that shooting that goddamned deer-in-a-dish down there was only the tip of the iceberg."

"Let's do it, then," Cletus said. "I've about had it with aliens and great horned gods, and if I don't get a shower soon I'm likely to end up as crazy as these three."

"You okay?" Bob asked, turning to the groggy, pale man they'd rescued.

"I don't really know," he said. "I'm Don, by the way. Don Watson. I think I owe you guys my life."

"You're welcome," Cletus said, "but we don't have time for this right now. You think you can walk?"

Don nodded. "I think so."

"Good," Bob cut in. "We'll call ahead for an ambulance and send the lot of you in to be looked at. Then we've got us one more stop to make before this is all over. Let's get going."

Earl and Jasper got Weston and David to their feet, groggy, wrists bound, but able to walk. Bob and Cletus supported Reverend Dozier on their shoulders and helped him limp out through the church to the trucks beyond. Don followed a bit more slowly. He was weak, but he was recovering quickly.

"Those men shot me!" Dozier whined. "They broke into my church and shot me in the foot."

"You can tell it to the judge," Bob muttered. "My bet is he'll ask them why they didn't aim for your head."

They tucked their three prisoners into the back of the Land Rover and let Don crawl in between Jasper and Earl, then left the parking lot in a shower of gravel, turning down the swamp road toward Old Mill and driving as fast as the bumpy road and darkness would allow.

Chapter Eleven

The drive back to Old Mill was fast, and quiet. Cletus kept glancing over his shoulder to make sure the three in the back were still restrained, and quiet, but there was no trouble. Even Reverend Dozier had given up on trying to harangue them into setting him free. Bob had told the man if he didn't shut up he'd get shot in his other foot, and that had done the trick.

As they neared Highway 17, Bob keyed up his radio and called ahead.

"Four-one to base, four-one to base. You there Colleen?"

The radio crackled, then Colleen's voice filled the Land Rover's cab.

"Read you fivers, four-one, copy?"

Bob took a deep breath, then replied.

"Listen closely, Colleen, I don't have much time. Get me an ambulance. Send it to the Lodge in Old Mill, and do it quick. I have the guy who was taken from the parking lot at The Cotton Gin – his name is Don Watson, and he is okay. I also have the men responsible – three prisoners. All of them will need to be looked at. I also need someone to keep the three in custody and make sure they stay put."

"Where have you been, Bob?" Colleen answered.

"Later Colleen. Later I'll fill you in on everything. Get Randy into a squad car and get him over to Old Mill. And get me that ambulance."

There was further sputtering on the other end of the line, but Bob put the microphone back in its cradle and drove on.

"Where are we going?" Dozier asked. "You aren't taking me to the hospital?"

"You'll get to the hospital," Bob growled, "if your own people don't kill us all first. We're going to Old Mill to put an end to this once and for all. Just shut up, sit back, and try not to bang your foot on the back of the seat. I imagine that would hurt."

As if in his words were prophetic, the Land Rover hit a last rut as they bounced up onto 17 and the good Reverend howled in pain. There hadn't been a word out of the twins since they'd been tucked into the back of the jeep. They didn't seem particularly upset; Cletus wondered if, for all their genius, they had a clue in the world of the trouble they were in.

It was dark, but the moon was still high in the sky. There were few lights on 17, mostly from homes, a couple of gas stations, and small real estate developments that had sprung up over the years, despite the ground being lower than water level during a big rain. Cotton fields stretched out on both sides of the road, white tips glittering in the moonlight. They had less than ten miles to go, but it seemed to take forever, and every thump of tire on asphalt felt like a huge clock ticking away toward some disaster he couldn't quite face.

Behind them, Jasper had Earl trying to reach Pap on the phone, but there was no answer. They tried the lodge, and they tried Jasper's home line, but all they got was a busy signal at the first number and the answering machine at the second. The road wound around past an old church, and the turn to Old Mill was finally in sight. Bob took it too fast, bringing the Land Rover up on two wheels, then back down with a jarring thump that brought another howl from Dozier. Jasper slowed and followed. Once they were around that corner, he knew even Bob was going to have to downshift, if he didn't want to go off the bridge and into the Perquimans River.

There was no traffic coming in, or out, of the town, and even in a sleepy place like Old Mill, this was strange. The twist through town was also known as Business 17, and there were several smaller roads that branched off in the center of town, stretching to towns up toward Virginia and West toward Greenville. Someone was always rolling along that dark narrow stretch, and the empty, barren road and moonlight tipped ripples on the river sent a shiver up Cletus' spine. Nothing about this night felt right, and even with Dozier and the twins tucked safely in the back of the Land Rover, he didn't feel safe. There had been a lot of trucks leaving Eternity, and he expected he was about to learn where they'd gone.

"What's that?" Bob grunted, pointing across Cletus' chest toward the center of town.

There was a bright, orange glow that could mean only one thing. Fire. There were no sirens, though, and that was also odd. Old Mill had a volunteer fire department that sported a brand new hook and ladder truck. Usually those boys were flying down the road if someone barbecued too enthusiastically, but whatever was going on tonight had apparently not caught their attention.

Bob picked up the microphone again, started to say something, then dropped it back in the cradle and floored the Land Rover with a curse. Cletus hung on and prayed they survived to be of some help in whatever was coming.

Old Mill had two main streets running perpendicular to 17. Bob turned at the first, ignoring the red light. He met no traffic going either way, and gunned it down Temple Street toward the lodge. Ahead, flames licked at the sky, and a dark black cloud of smoke rose to blot the sky. There were bodies moving in and out of those clouds as well, lots of them. Cletus leaned out the window, trying to get a better look, but smoke wafted across the road and obscured his view.

"Slow down, Bob," he called out. "Jesus, whoever's in the road up there, you're going to knock them to hell and back."

Bob slowed, but he didn't look happy about it. In fact, he looked like nothing would give him more pleasure than to plow ahead into whatever lay ahead, drive straight through it, and out the other side. Maybe if he did, he'd just keep going and never come back to this craziness that had been his town only a few short hours before.

Bob cursed and pulled into the parking lot near the courthouse. Jasper pulled in behind, and moments later, the first sirens rose behind them. Cletus turned and saw Deputy Randy Barstow hurtling down the road in a cruiser. Randy was a bit over-enthusiastic in the performance of his duties, and normally Bob would have wanted anyone but his least favorite hothead on the job, but this was different. As Randy pulled up, Bob through him the keys to the Land Rover.

"Take them," he said. "Ambulance should be here soon. You follow along with them, make sure they are all taken care of, and make sure they are locked up tighter than a virgin's knees when you're done. You understand me, Randy?"

The younger man stared down the street, dumbfounded, watching men and women moving in and out of the smoke.

"The fire…" he said.

"Damn the fire," Bob growled, shaking him. "Get these boys to the hospital Randy. I'll take care of the fire. "And watch them. They're kidnappers, and probably murderers to boot. You don't want to give them an inch, you hear?"

Don walked up then, and Bob glanced at him distractedly, as if just remembering he was there.

"Randy," he called out. The deputy turned back.

"See that this man gets taken care of too, and call the Troopers. He's the guy that was abducted from the Cotton Gin. He's probably hungry, and I don't want anything happening to him."

"Yes sir," Randy replied. Apparently the deputy had gathered the seriousness of what was happening and was stepping up to the plate.

"Good damn deal," Cletus muttered. He stared at the hazy smoke where the lodge should have been, and something flickered. He couldn't quite make out what it was, but the urge to know was overwhelming. He started forward, not paying any further attention to Bob, or the others around him.

Meanwhile, Randy and Don climbed into the Land Rover and Randy stepped out to wave down the ambulance as it turned into the parking lot, attracted by Bob's flashing lights. Bob watched for a moment longer, then turned toward the fire and the smoke.

Cletus was already headed toward the lodge at a trot. He'd meant to wait for Bob, but something in the glow from the flames and the shifting, snaking clouds of smoke drew him forward. He heard Bob call out to him, but he didn't turn. He stepped off the sidewalk and crossed temple. He pulled his shirt up over his mouth and nose, using the material as an inefficient filter, and squatted low.

The smoke was thicker than he'd expected, and he closed his eyes at the sting. It was a mistake. The moment the dim light was cut off, his boot caught on something and he tripped. Cletus cursed and waved his arms, reached out to break his fall, and landed hard. Something cut his hand, and his knees buried in soft soil. He opened his eyes and stared at the overturned earth, and the cotton plant gouging his palm.

The street was gone. He knelt in the dirt, and though the smoke had cleared some, the first blazed as bright as ever, dead ahead. It rose to the sky, and he saw the men and women of Old Mill, stretching into the distance, lined up on both sides of that fire like fence posts, guiding him forward.

Cletus turned, wild-eyed, and looked back the way he'd come. There was nothing there. The field stretched off into the distance where a line of trees was silhouetted against the skyline. He staggered to his feet and rubbed his eyes, hoping his sight would clear, but nothing changed. Hundreds of eyes watched him, lined up and waiting, and he took a step forward, then another. As he closed on the bizarre, impossible fire, he heard their voices, chanting low and steady.

He reached the first of those lined up waiting, and he scanned their faces. He knew some of them. They were men and women he'd known all his life, barbers and farmers, the kid who bagged his beer and groceries over at the grocery – and others. He didn't speak – something in their eyes told him they would not listen – that possibly they wouldn't even hear. Their lips moved in unison, and the chant grew deeper and more powerful as he passed through their ranks, approaching the fire.

Beyond the flames a huge form flickered in the shadows. Branches twined and rippled like snakes, stretching up toward the heavens. As he drew nearer, the shape rose over him, immense and dark. He knew the shape, but it was too large, the proportions were wrong. The totem had been tall when he'd seen it last, but now it seemed to touch the sky.

She stood waiting for him, and though his mind screamed at him to recoil from her, conjuring images of Nettie's wrinkled face and clawed hands, he could not pull away. Instead, he stepped forward and, smiling, she opened her arms to him again.

Then another stepped from the crowd, and he nearly blacked out. It was Nettie – old as she'd appeared on the porch of the old shack, old as she'd been since he'd known her as a child, old as his father claimed she must always have been. The girl he held squirmed in his embrace, pressing herself to him and others gathered near.

Arms slid around him and nimble, urgent fingers plucked at the buttons of his shirt. His belt slid off and though he cried out softly in negation, the girl drew him forward and he stepped free of the clothing. Other hands stripped her simple gown, and she was beautiful.

A musky, heady scent filled the air and his body responded. She gripped him and he felt like stone in her supple fingers. She pulled him forward and fell back and he tumbled into her. He gazed into her eyes and they were wild, her lips parted and her back arched. He drove forward, burying himself in wet, moist flesh. She swallowed him, shivering up and down, pressing her shoulder blades and the balls of her feet into the wood of the table. The heat of the fire seared his back and sweat coated every inch of his body. He growled, unable to breathe without drawing more of the foul air into his lungs. It smelled of the forest, the swamp, the stables and so many other things at once he couldn't sort them out in his mind, and all the time he tried, he drove deeper and deeper into the writhing flesh beneath him.

When he climaxed, he couldn't see. His chest was on fire, and his breath seemed too thick to pass. He toppled to the side and cried out. Above him, he saw the totem, antlers dark and ropy against the sky. Carved wooden eyes glared down at him and glowed with an inner illumination.

Nettie stood over him. He saw that, old and frail as she was, she held the girl's body in her arms. She smiled at him and – in that moment – her face took on a beauty he could not comprehend. Then, she stepped over him, and was gone.

His next lungful of air was blistering smoke. He heard a voice calling his name, and he rolled, trying to get back to his feet. He felt wood beneath his fingers, and it was hot. His thoughts reeled, and he tried to press up off the floor. He made it to his knees. His eyes burned, but he lifted his gaze.

Above him the ancient wood of the totem burned crazily. The deer's head was wreathed in flames that danced up the antlers toward the ceiling above. He blinked, and then his mind cleared. The lodge. He was in the lodge, and…

Strong hands gripped him under his armpits and yanked him backward. Cletus fought feebly. He tried to scramble to his feet, but more hands joined the first set, and whoever it was dragged him backward, bumping him along the floor. He felt splinters stab into his flesh, and he cried out, but the sound died in a cough that stole his breath. He tried one more time to scream, but the effort was more than his tortured flesh could take, and he slipped over the edge into darkness. The last thing he saw was the deer totem engulfed in flame and the antlers, crumbling into a cloud of black ash as they fell.

When Cletus came to, he was lying on his back staring up at the sky. Bob was leaning over him, and others stood near, Pap included, staring down at him like they thought he was already dead. He shook his head slowly, regretted it, then managed to part his parched lips.

"Bob?" he said. The word was too soft, and he coughed roughly at the effort.

Bob leaned closer. "Lie still, Cletus," he said. "There's time to talk later, and believe me, you're going to tell me just what in hell happened in there. The last thing I saw was you walking off into the smoke."

Cletus turned his head and saw the black smoke still rising. Fire trucks were on the street now, and plumes of water arched into the air to fall sizzling on the flames. Cletus let his head fall back, and he closed his eyes. When they didn't open again, Bob checked for a pulse, found it strong, and stood up.

The ambulance siren rose for the second time in an hour, and he stepped to the curb to wave it down. In the back of the crowd gathered and watching from a distance, an old woman with wispy gray hair stood very still. Her expression was serene, and her lip curled in an enigmatic smile.

Chapter Twelve

Cletus typed the last few words of his article, read back over what he'd written, and clicked "save" to preserve the work. The article was a long one, filled with references to things that hadn't actually happened, but that made good copy. There were photos imbedded in the text – the twins, Jasper and Pap, the burned lodge, and the cellar laboratory. It should have been big news, and Cletus knew that better than anyone, but the bigger papers had turned away from it in horror. Even if it was true, how could they present such a fanciful pile of crap to the reading public?

In the end, the news agencies had reported an abduction, and had managed to ID the first 'victim' as well. They chalked it all up to craziness in Eternity, including hazy details about a cult and mutilation, but neglecting to mention that the first dead man had apparently begun to heal with Bambi's head slapped onto his neck, or that another such head had lived a short life in a Petri dish beneath the First Church of Light and Starry Wisdom.

Reverend Dozier was on his way to jail for a long time, along with the twins, who Cletus was certain would end up locked away in some government lab, working on things Cletus didn't want to know about and finishing one another's sentences. It was how things worked – no one was going to toss away genius over a little genetic experimentation. Hadn't that same government slipped Nazi scientists into the US after WWII?

At the top of the article the byline read:
Cletus J. Diggs & Earl Suggs
The article wasn't likely to launch Earl into a literary career, but it had made the big man happy, and for blowing the crap out of Bambi the Zombie , he deserved it. Besides, the story was featured in the Weekly Globe Examiner, bumping even the doctored photograph

of a giant grasshopper held up by its back legs and displayed by a grinning West Virginia farmer. It was big time, and it helped pay the bills. Cletus was all about paying the bills.

Jasper had his arm in a sling from where he tumbled down the stairs, and Pap was still getting his wind back. His story was almost as strange as Cletus' own. He and about a dozen others, thanks to the call from Earl's phone, had holed up in the lodge and they were there when the trucks from Eternity showed up and started parking in a circle around the place. None of them seemed to know for sure when the fire started, but Pap was certain it began outside. He clearly remembered a ring of fire around the entire building and smoke so thick they thought they'd never get out.

In the end, it was like a corridor opened up in the flames, leading out the door. That was how Cletus had made it in, and how those inside had gotten out. Miraculously, no one had been seriously injured. Cletus still had trouble drawing a deep breath without coughing. The smoke had burned his lungs, and he still had a couple of raw patches on his arms and legs from the heat. All in all, he figured he'd gotten off pretty easy.

Bob had been given a citation by the Governor of NC for bravery, and for solving the abduction case. He'd been damned close-mouthed about the details of the investigation and the rescue in Eternity. He took credit for Earl's shot through the Good Reverend Dozier's foot, claiming the prisoner had tried to escape. Bob said he'd warned the man to stop, but had been forced to take a non-deadly shot when Dozier dove toward his window. No one questioned this, particularly since Bob had eyewitnesses, and the only detractor was Dozier himself.

All around three counties, hunters were resting easier, though there had been a decided drop in sales of hunting and taxidermy supplies. The Harvest festival had come and gone, a muted, calm affair that hardly raised a social blip. Cletus did not attend, nor did Jasper. They stayed in and watched a race on Cletus' TV, washing remnants of soot and ash from their systems with cold, cheap beer.

Despite all of this, something haunted Cletus, and he knew that writing the last words in the article wasn't going to change that. There were things left unfinished, and there was no time like the present for taking care of business. He turned off his computer, stood, and headed for the door, and his truck beyond. On his way past the table, he grabbed a brown paper bag, gripping it where it was twisted around the neck of a bottle of Jim Beam.

The shack was just as he remembered it. The table was bare – no glasses, and no trace of the bottle he'd brought the time before. Cletus climbed out of his truck and stepped up onto the creaky porch, placing the bottle in the center of the table and looking around carefully at the old home, and the woods beyond. It was late afternoon; he hadn't been willing to come at night, but somehow he didn't believe anyone would be 'home' if he came at noon. It was the closest compromise he could make.

This time the sense of urgency was displaced by one of inevitability. He didn't need to be anywhere in particular. He'd brought his own glass, as well, so he didn't have to wait to begin drinking. There was plenty of courage in the Beam bottle to get him through the evening, he thought, and if nothing else came of it, he'd be drunk, and that would be enough.

As it turned out, he didn't have long to wait. He poured a double shot into the first of the two tumblers he'd brought, placed it on the table, and filled the second halfway. He took a quick gulp, and gazed out at the woods, watching the sun set slowly toward their leafy peaks.

Her voice nearly made him spill his drink.

"I knew you'd come," Nettie said softly.

Cletus didn't turn at first. He continued to watch the sunset, and he took another, longer pull on his drink. He didn't really know why he'd come. He didn't have any clearly formed questions, and he figured it would be best just to let her lead him wherever it was she was planning to take him and get it over with.

Finally, her silence drew him in.

"Why did you help me?" he asked. "Dozier could have brought back your horned monstrosity out in Eternity…"

"What he was creating was an abomination," she said softly. "You know that. You can't build a God in your basement, and every time you try, you end up with less – and more – than you bargained for. "

"You helped him too," Cletus pointed out.

"To a point," she said. "It's a matter of belief, Cletus – what do you believe? I remember a time when men and women knew the importance of the old ways. The Great Horned one walked the swamp through the power of their minds and their dreams. He fed on their faith, and in turn he gave them children, and crops – far more and stronger than anything that exists today. You smelled him – I know you did. You saw him in that fire, too – but it wasn't a stick, buried in the corner of the building you saw – he is much greater than that – much more powerful, even now that the belief has faded. He's almost lost to us, you know. It won't be long before the world moves on, and leaves him a dusty shadow in the swamp."

"We slowed that down," Cletus said.

He turned, and he saw that she nodded. Her glass was empty, and he filled it again.

"There's folks now, for a while, that will believe," she went on. "No one that knows what it is they are believing in, exactly, but even those strange, pale boys in Eternity helped. No one who saw what they created will ever forget it. No one who watched that fire, or worshipped with Reverend Dozier, will be able to erase it from their memories, and they'll pass it on, weakened and distorted, but they'll tell the tales, and he'll walk a few years longer. It's all I can do – I'm a very old woman, and I'm tired."

Cletus stared at his drink. He wanted to ask at least one more question, but he didn't know how to word it. A creaking floorboard broke the spell of the moment, and he glanced up.

Behind Nettie, a young woman stood. She as young, no more than twenty. Her hair was so platinum blonde it nearly matched the nimbus of gray surrounding Nettie's ancient, wizened face. She watched Cletus with wide, unblinking eyes. She neither smiled, nor frowned. Her hands rested protectively on Nettie's shoulders. Then she stepped up beside the table, and Cletus saw the bulge of her belly. She was with child – far along from the look of it. He grew pale and gulped what was left of his whiskey.

Nettie started laughing. "Yes, Cletus, you are a part of this now. He worked through you, and the line that I have been a part of will pass on through the generations. You'll feel him if you stand too long in the fields, or if you spend too much time fishing in the swamp. He'll watch over you – he's part of you now, as you are part of…the future."

Nettie reached out and laid her hand gently on the girl's swollen belly.

Cletus shuddered. His fears that he'd lain with Nettie had been replaced by a deep-rooted, chilling sensation of connection to a darkness he couldn't see. He suddenly felt as if the shadows the rising moon had spread across the road and his truck were not all the product of light and limb, but cast instead by antlers, branching up and away into the night sky. The air thickened, just for a moment, and he smelled the musky, rutting odor of animals and the scent of fresh mown grass and fields at harvest.

He stood quickly and stumbled toward the steps with a cry. He caught himself on the rickety railing, glanced back, and saw that the table was bare. No one sat across it; both bottles and glasses were gone.

He hurried to his truck and slid in behind the wheel, checking to be certain all the doors were locked and the windows tightly closed. Then he sat, steadied his breath and his heartbeat, and started the engine.

Backing slowly, he aimed the truck at the road, and the highway beyond. As he pulled away, he couldn't shake the sensation of eyes watching him from the shadows and a powerful, hovering presence just outside the groping limits of his mind.

Special Bonus Story!

The Not Quite Right Reverend Cletus J. Diggs
& The Fruit of Another Vine

This story was originally written for the lettered edition of the original limited print edition of this novella. The names of many of the characters are those of lettered subscribers to Bad Moon Books – I thank them all for buying my book, and I dedicate this story to them. If you are ever driving between Hertford, North Carolina and Elizabeth City, down Highway 17, you may see the vine that grows up one of the telephone poles in the shape of a woman. She holds a gun, and she still aims it off over that redneck ranch house into the trees. Who knows what she has in her sites?

The Not Quite Right Reverend Cletus J. Diggs & the Fruit of another Vine

The Day that Geoff Guthrie died, a whole lot of folks began breathing easier. It wasn't that Geoff wasn't well liked; he was. It wasn't that he'd lived a bad life, or that he deserved what he got, because nobody deserved that. Sheriff Bob over in Old Mill deputized three new men that day, Jim Pepper, Keith Prochaska, and Jason Bell, and dragged out a whole pickup truck load of forensic equipment that hadn't been used in a long time, but no one expected anything to come of it.

Cletus Jehosephat Diggs was among those with low expectations. First off, the only man whose heart was into the investigation was Bob. The others were along for the money and the chance to turn on the siren in one of the county cars. They didn't really want to go within a mile of Geoff Guthrie's place, and they sure didn't want to go poking around before Liz Scott cleared out her stuff. The courts had been pretty clear; though it hardly seemed fair. Geoff Guthrie had never finalized his divorce from his estranged wife, Wanda, so on his death, his property reverted to her. Didn't matter that Liz had been living with him the last eight years, taking care of him, getting him off to work and making sure Wanda didn't run him down on the street out of spite.

Of course, it wasn't Geoff Guthrie that was really the problem. It was his father. Old Roy had sown oats as wild as any ever sown, and he paid the price, in the end. Some said he got off easy. He died of cancer. Roy had health insurance, but it wasn't much, and it wasn't enough. It never is. Some said it was the water from his well that killed him – which he knew to be bad but was too lazy to filter it or call Culligan. Cletus had other ideas, and he also thought, since it wasn't likely Bob was going to uncover anything important, that it was about time he looked into it.

Geoff Guthrie had been found dead in his pickup truck, listening to a Buck Owens tape out front of his home. No one had seen a thing. There was a single bullet hole through his forehead. No sign of a struggle, but he was dead as a doornail, and things like that just don't happen often near Old Mill. Most folks in Perquimans County shoot squirrels and deer.

The Weekly Globe would love a piece on the Guthrie killing, particularly in light of the back story. Cletus would have been over to Geoff's trailer already, but he was as wary of both Liz and Wanda as any man. He'd had his own moments with Wanda and had thankfully cut it short prior to the commencement of stalking. With Bob running around the place distracting everyone, Cletus figured to get in, snap some pertinent photos, and then hit the streets and gather the story. He didn't much care if he figured out who killed Geoff Guthrie, but he wanted his back story straight. Some folks called the Globe a tabloid, but Cletus was a journalist. He started with the facts and only embellished if the satellite TV was about to be cut off.

The funeral services had been set to take place at the Old Mill Presbyterian Church the following Sunday. Geoff Guthrie was not a Presbyterian, and Reverend Roberts had been quick to point this out when the family came to him about holding forth over the services. The family was adamant. The Presbyterian Church had a large, spacious lawn for the services, where there could be a proper viewing. They also had a parking lot accessible from both sides with a possible third egress across the hill in back. Considering that all the women in Geoff Guthrie and Roy's lives might show up, not to mention whoever else Geoff might have pissed off, folks wanted to be sure they had their exit routes planned in advance.

It was crazy, and crazy was what Cletus thrived on. People in New York and San Francisco loved reading about the goings on in rural North Carolina and the crazier those goings on got, the better. Cletus has been secretly relieved when Reverend Larry Roberts got the nod, because, as an ordained minister, and the only one likely to stand at a pulpit with a shotgun in his hand, Cletus had been afraid that Geoff's family might call him. Then he'd have had to hire a photographer and written under a different byline.

Cletus watched from down the street until Bob and his new deputies had loaded their equipment and pulled out onto the winding road toward the highway. He tailed them at a safe distance. It wasn't like they were going to lose him. He knew right where they were headed and likely as not Bob knew Cletus was following. There was only one road out of town, unless you wanted to curve around and cross the river bridge.

Geoff had lived in a trailer he was converting to a ranch style home. What that meant in southeastern North Carolina was that he'd tied together two double-wides in an "L" shape and was fixin' to have Casper & McLeod Construction come in and brick-face the whole thing. The locals had taken to calling it the Double L Ranch and Cletus thought that would work just fine for his story. Geoff Guthrie had been doing alright for himself, and he'd intended to fix his place up right before he left it to his son, Norm. Now all of that was in question. Norm was Geoff's by Liz. The courts and old Judge Berke were going to have to sort that one out, but as likely as not, still being a minor, Norm would get some cash, and Wanda would get the home.

Being spring, everything was green, growing and blooming. Cars were yellow with pollen and bees flew around fat and drunk with it, so overloaded they could barely keep themselves airborne. About a quarter of a mile from Geoff's place, Cletus pulled to the side of the road and stared. There was a power pole leaning at a slight angle over the ditch, providing air conditioning and cable TV to Geoff's kingdom. Steel cables braced that pole, snaking down to the ground on either side. A heavy shielded cable crossed the ditch to the trailer.

Vines had started at the base of the pole and twined their way upward. It was a common sight near Old Mill. Sometimes the vines wound themselves into odd shapes. There was a telephone pole a mile back toward Old Mill that looked like Bigfoot shambling off across the field when the sun started to fade. Above Geoff's place, something different had formed.

The vines had formed into the shape of a very tall woman, and she was either pointing at, or reaching for, the crime scene. She leaned out over the ditch, arm extended toward the trailers as if beseeching them, or ready to snatch something up and take it. One leg was bent at the knee, and her hair flowed out behind her like it was caught in the wind. Cletus sat and stared for a while.

Bob and his boys were already parked and had started into Geoff's place. Cletus reached for the folder on the seat beside him. He opened it and pulled out an old photograph. He held it up to the windshield of his truck so he could see it, side by side with the eerie, green profile of the vine woman.

"Holy shit," he said. "I'll be double-D goddamned."

The woman in the portrait was named Paula Beauchamp, and she'd been missing for nearly fifteen years. She'd lived alone since her husband Mark ran head-on into a herd of deer on Simpson's Ditch Road and died with an eight-point buck's prize rack buried in the top of his skull. She was dead too, most likely, but officially listed as missing, and had been ever since ol' Roy called it in.

The disappearance had never been solved. Some folks thought Roy killed her. Others like Andrew Simmons down at the barber shop and Bob Jackson who pumped gas down in Winfall said she was too much woman for Roy and she took off. Allegedly she crawled out of Roy's bed early one morning and headed off to work. She waited tables at Walter Danenhower's place in Elizabeth City, and she had to get an early start. She stopped by Chris Hansen's gas station about 6:30 and topped off her tank. Two boys, Douglas McDade and Leigh Haig, who hung out at the station saw her there. They commented on her skirt, and Roy confirmed the clothing.

That's where things got hazy. She never made it to work that day, and she never came back. Her old Ford had been found two counties away at the end of a road. A dead end road. There were probably a few thousand roads in rural North Carolina where the road sign simply said Dead End. It was no surprise it had become a self-fulfilling prophecy. Roy got the car back, but he never heard from Paula Beauchamp again, and as they love to do, folks had started talking.

Cletus had heard a dozen versions of how Paula met her end. Roy was posited as everything from an axe murderer to a pedophile who drove her away and ditched her to protect his own sordid secrets. None of it was ever proved. The troopers had come in and run an investigation. They'd been everywhere from Phil Fritz's feed store to the coffee shop where Paul Worosello had been serving sludge since the Great Depression, but no one knew anything. Roy lived outside town, and Paula worked all the way in Elizabeth City. Folks in Old Mill kept mostly to themselves, and unless you asked old Bill Woodward the postmaster, you'd be hard pressed to find anyone who knew more than a dozen people they weren't related to outside a five mile radius of their home.

It wasn't facts that made folks talk. "Domestic disturbances," as Sheriff Bob liked to call them, were the norm in Old Mill. No matter that it had been Bob's daddy, "Big Bob" who was sheriff at the time. Most things never really change. No one would have gotten worked up at all if it hadn't been for that damned vine woman pointing at the trailer every summer. She looked like she had something to say, and there wasn't much doubt who – or at least what – she was pointing at. One year they had an article about the situation – Mike Caouette wrote it up for the Old Mill Town Crier. They tried to tie it back to Blackbeard, who it's said spent some time running up and down the rivers near the swamp, but that line of thought didn't go too far.

The only thing that came of it, in fact, was that the sheriff had to haul Kevin Locke and Jason Houghton in for questioning when a bunch of holes showed up in Geoff's backyard. They'd figured that if Blackbeard was behind the haunted vine on the power pole, the woman must be pointing toward a treasure. All those boys found was the two year old remnant of Roy's Beagle, Bocephus, and a pit full of rusted out beer cans that'd been buried after a party years back.

In the end, Kevin Locke and Jason Houghton got citations for vandalism, and Geoff Guthrie, who was pretty pissed off at the time, got cited for burying garbage on country ground. No further mention was made of the woman on the pole, but Cletus had kept a record. Every spring, and every fall, he took pictures. He had a small gallery of shots of the eerie, pointing figure. He'd drawn angles and lines to try and pinpoint the exact spot she was pointing at, but at other times he was convinced she was reaching out to grab something, or to touch someone. He'd done some research out at Josef Hernandez Community College – trying to find stories of possessed vines, or haunted plants, but there wasn't much to go on.

Now he stared at the photo in his hand and wondered how in the hell he'd managed never to notice it before.

Cletus tucked the photo back into the folder on the seat beside him and grabbed his camera. No time like the present, but he didn't see any reason to drive closer and call attention to himself. Best to be in there and clicking away before Bob noticed. Easier to say you're sorry, and all that. Besides, it was a nice day, and he wanted a closer look at the pole, and the vines.

When he reached the base of it, he turned and followed the stretching arm with his gaze. He looked at the yard, and the trailer. For some reason he couldn't have explained later, he glanced up over the house as well. Behind it, cotton fields stretched into the distance, and a line of trees. Far back in those trees, something glinted.

It was probably a trick of light – it had to be right? That glint of light half-blinded Cletus, leaving a brilliant after trail, and when he instinctively turned away from it…the trail led to the fingertip of the woman looming overhead. Cletus gasped and stepped back, nearly dropping his camera. He shook his head, cleared his eyes, and frowned. Then, without thinking about the wisdom of giving up the shots he'd hoped to get at the old Double L Ranch, he stepped out into the cotton field and started across, headed for the trees.

The field was wider than it had looked from the road, but Cletus had spent his share of time in the fields, and he hardly noticed. When he reached the midpoint, he caught another glimpse of whatever was glittering. He swerved and headed straight for it, picking up his pace. He wanted to get across the field without being noticed, if possible. Whatever was there, he wanted some time to figure it out before he shared with anyone, and he was probably trespassing.

As he passed beyond the tree line, he glanced back over his shoulder. There was no sign of Bob or his new charges, and that was good. Probably they were still inside – investigating – and it seemed none of them had noticed Cletus passing around and behind them.

He hurried his steps, and was surprised, after a few yards, to find a trail. It hadn't been used in a while. Cletus frowned. He'd been certain the trees would only run a short ways and then break out into another field, but it seemed that this forested area stretched back a ways – at least half a mile. He tried to situate the far side of the trees in his mind and figure out where they might end on the other side, but it was oddly disorienting, and he gave it up. Didn't matter.

He followed the rough trail a few hundred yards in, and it was then he spotted the shack. It was old, canted over to one side with boards half-loose from the frame and only about half its roof intact. The shingles had curled up and looked as if some huge beast had ripped them out nails and all, leaving only the skeletal structure of the roof remained.

Cletus stopped and snapped a picture of the place. He had no idea why, but it seemed important. Then he started forward slowly. Cletus had lived in Old Mill all his life, but this was out of town. He didn't remember any stories about families living out here – and from the look of the place, no one had lived there in fifty years or more, but it felt off somehow. The door stood ajar and hung half off the hinges. Wooden shutters covered the ruins of the windows in front, and he assumed it was the same all the way around. The wood was green with mold and rotted.

Cletus followed the walk up to the old porch and climbed the steps carefully. Every time he moved he expected to fall through and break a leg, but the old wood held. It was very quiet back in those trees, and that felt odd too. There should have been some damned birds, or a squirrel skittering out under his feet, but there was nothing. He knew he should back out and go get Bob. If there was something inside worth finding, it was probably going to be a crime scene.

"Ah hell," he muttered.

Cletus stepped forward and into the old shack. He let the camera dangle so he'd have his hands free if he needed them.

There was only one main room. In the rear he saw a door leading into a small enclosure in the corner – a closet? There was a table, a rotten wooden bench, and some unidentifiable lumps and piles leaned against the walls. None of it mattered. Cletus stood and stared at the single chair across the table from him. He heard a horrible, strangled sound and backed away – then realized the sound was his own, and he remembered to breathe.

His legs didn't want to hold him up, but Cletus knew he was

going to have to get the photograph. He raised the camera, snapped off a shot, checked the digital window and cursed. His hands were shaking. He gritted his teeth and focused carefully.

The woman's skeletal arm pointed straight through the camera lens into Cletus' soul, and beyond. It pointed straight back at the Double L Ranch, and that power pole. Like the two were reaching out to hold hands. She had long, dark hair, at least the straggling remnant of it was black. She was slumped over the table as if she might have fallen asleep, but Cletus was pretty certain it had been more than that.

He snapped a couple of pictures, took a deep breath, and stepped forward again. There wasn't much of a smell, after so many years. Unless he was completely off – it had been fifteen. Something was wrong, though. Even in her decomposed state, she didn't resemble his mental image of Paula Beauchamp. He thought she was too short. He carefully stepped up to the table, knowing Bob was likely going to run him in for disturbing a crime scene, but unable to look away.

On the table, under the bones of one hand, a piece of paper rested. Cletus leaned in and read through the dust, trying to fill in letters where mold and insects had ruined the paper.

"He was mine. I didn't have much, but he was mine. If he finds you, I hope he gags on the smell trying to get back that ring.
Paula"

Cletus glanced at the other hand. The one that was outstretched over the table pointing at the Double L and the road beyond. On the ring finger, wrapped now like a loose collar on a stick in the mud, rested a gold ring. In the center was a diamond setting. It wasn't expensive, or nice, but it was a diamond, and somehow, though the idea was ludicrous, Cletus knew it was what he'd seen. Somehow the sunlight had filtered through the trees, through cracked plank walls or broken shutters, and struck that diamond. It had glittered as if summoning him. As if the woman on the pole were pointing the way – as if he was meant to see.

He shook off these thoughts quickly and snapped a couple more shots. Then, without a word or another glance at the interior of that shack, he backed out the door, stepped off the porch, and lit off for the road, and his car. Numb as his mind was, it was working on one level. The basest level. He knew he had to get his camera back to his truck and tucked away before Bob saw him. If the sheriff thought he had pictures of what he was about to turn over, they'd be confiscated, and the story would slip away.

He stumbled through the cotton toward the road, fighting for his balance, and to retain his breakfast. The image of the rotted corpse haunted him, and he was having a hard time concentrating on getting one foot in front of the next. Somehow he reached the road without being spotted, and opened the passenger side door of his truck. He slid the camera off his neck and tucked it up under the seat, and then he closed the door and headed back toward the trailer, Sheriff Bob, and the deputies.

When he glanced up at the woman on the pole, she seemed to have lost definition. Somehow, she seemed less like a woman. Vines shot out where he hadn't noticed them before, and the symmetry of the legs and the pointing arm was not quite right. It looked more like a clump of vines than a woman. Cletus wondered what he'd see when he looked at his photos later on.

As he walked down the drive toward the Double L, Keith Prochaska saw him and waved.

"Hey Cletus," he said. "What are you doing here?"

"Get Bob," Cletus said. "I've got something to show him, and he isn't going to like it."

Then Cletus leaned against the side of the house, closed his eyes, and waited.

The body turned out not to be Paula, who remained missing. There was another woman, a dancer from The Cotton Gin out by Elizabeth City. She'd disappeared about the same time as Paula, but no one thought anything of it. Dancers came and went pretty regularly. Everyone figured she'd just headed back up to Virginia, where she was going to college during the day, and gotten a job at a club closer to school. What Cletus hadn't seen, since she was lying across the table, face down was that she'd been shot one time – in the forehead.

Sheriff Bob had to talk to every oldster in the county, but he managed to piece it together eventually. Roy had been seeing the dancer, Susie Lee Tanner, on the side. It had been pretty serious, and one geezer, a fellow by the name of Mike Bodak, had been tending bar the night Roy proposed.

Apparently, Roy had tried to tell Paula and let her down gently. He must have had Susie Lee out in that shack, waiting for Paula to go to work. Somehow Paula found out. She made a stop by the shack on her way out of town, and never looked back. Maybe Roy went out there and saw what happened, then just let it go and hoped no one would find out. Maybe he just figured he'd been dumped and stood up on the same day. Any way you looked at it, he lived for fifteen years within sight of his fiancée's final resting place and no one was ever the wiser.

The photos were the same as his last glimpse of the pole. There was a vague resemblance to a woman if you screwed your eyes up just right, but mostly it looked like a tangle of vines, pointing nowhere. Cletus asked others about it, but their memories had faded, or they were in denial. Everyone sort of remembered the woman and the pole, but no one could really bring the image to mind.

Bob wrapped up his investigation. He couldn't prove who'd fired the shot that killed Geoff Guthrie, and he was tired of people asking him if he thought there was a connection to the other shooting. He made a half-assed sweep of the area, looking for an older woman resembling Paula, but nothing came of that either. Most folks believed Geoff Guthrie was shot by his ex, but she didn't own a gun, and no one was admitting to loaning her one. The shot had come from a deer rifle. The slug was imbedded in the back of the truck.

As it turned out neither Liz nor Wanda wanted the Double L after hearing about what had been out back for so long. It was put up for sale, the proceeds to be split between Wanda and the son, Norm. Cletus wrote his story, and since it wasn't going to work without it, he used Photoshop to bring the woman on the pole back to life.

As he typed the last word, saved the file and got ready to e-mail it to his editor, he hesitated. Just for a moment, it felt like someone might be pointing at him, and he wondered what really happened to Paula. Why had her car been abandoned? Who was behind the woman on the pole – was it a blast from Purgatory, a last-ditch effort to make things right.

He imagined another photo, the entire wooded area on fire and huge demonic face embedded in the smoke. Then he grinned, attached his files, and hit send.

"May she rest in peace, wherever the hell she is," he muttered. "Amen."

SPECIAL FREE NOVEL PREVIEW

The Not Quite Right Reverend
Cletus J. Diggs

&

THE CRAZY CASE OF FOREMAN JAMES

Chapter One

Foreman James was a special child. That's what his momma told him, and he heard it sometimes in church, or outside the market. Foreman didn't feel special, but he knew he wasn't the sharpest arrow in the quiver—which was something his aunt Ida told him when no one was around. She also said that a well-aimed arrow could do fine, sharp or dull. That being the case, he supposed if all those smart people said he was special, it must be so.

When Josiah White offered him a job sweeping up around the peanut oil factory, he was happy to have it. If at no other time, he felt special in his work shirt and boots, pushing shells off the work floor or carrying out boxes and bags to be hauled to the dump and burned.

He took his money home to his mother, who worked long hours at the cotton mill for too little pay. He didn't make much, but every little bit helped. His mother had told him that his daddy went north to find work, but that he'd come home one day. Still, things had been tight. That was what his mother said. Foreman didn't know what she meant, exactly, though he had some jeans that were too tight, and that hurt when he wore them, so he understood that tight wasn't good. No matter what happened, there was always food on the table, and he had a warm place to sleep. There were others Foreman knew who were not so lucky.

The men who worked at the peanut oil factory were a rough bunch. Foreman kept his distance whenever possible...they usually didn't hurt him, but they could be mean. The factory provided very little in the way of entertainment, and they took their laughs where they could get them.

"You just keep to yourself and do your work," his momma said. "Don't pay them no mind. Lord knows they wouldn't know what to do with it."

It helped that he genuinely liked to do things with his hands and to be busy. He liked to eat his apple and bread down beside the huge old oak down by the river…and he liked the way he felt important when he stood in line to pick up his pay each Friday. He always carried it very carefully straight home, and when he handed that money to his momma, he felt like he mattered.

Foreman was a quiet boy, and he tried, whenever possible, to melt into the background. Sometimes he saw and heard things. People didn't notice him, and as often as not, even if they did see him, they dismissed him without a thought.

"He's as simple as a Billy Goat," they'd say. "He wouldn't remember his name if it wasn't sewn on his shirt."

And a lot of times it was true. He had a hard time concentrating on things outside his Ettal routine. If he went to the market he had to have a written list. If they gave him a new job at the factory, it often took him several days to commit the new steps of his schedule to memory. Still, he was steady and hard-working. Once he had a thing set in his mind, he didn't forget.

It didn't bother him that things came hard. His momma had once told him it was a blessing. Most folks went through life fretting over things that he never gave a second thought to. He reckoned it must be true, because not fretting over things he couldn't remember came natural to him. He liked to keep to himself, and he liked others to keep to themselves.

It was a day like that, a day when he was working quietly behind the large peanut oil vats that he overheard Jarrod Pope talking to Billy White. Jarrod was a big man, with a very red face. Foreman didn't like him because every time the man came near he got a big grin on his face that had no humor behind it. Jarrod was foreman at the plant—his father, Josiah, owned it, along with half the county.

Jarrod liked to smack Foreman on the back hard enough to hurt while pretending the two were friends. He would take Foreman's hat, throw trash where Foreman had just cleaned up, and ask questions about Foreman's mother that made him feel like he'd turned as red as Jarrod himself.

This day, Jarrod didn't see him, nor did Billy. They were leaned in close to one another and talking excitedly.

Foreman tried not to listen. He didn't want to know what

they were talking about. If they caught him, they'd accuse him of eavesdropping. If they were talking about a woman, Foreman would blush and likely bang into something and give himself away. He wished they would just go back to work.

"I'm telling you," Jarrod said, "that is one hot little lady. You should have seen her. Hell, I tried to tell her I couldn't do that to Jake, but she wouldn't listen. She was all over me."

"That don't sound like Alice," Billy said. "Hell, Jarrod, I've known her since she was six. She's been with Jake since high school. Besides, I thought you had eyes for Mandy Winslow."

"You calling me a liar, Billy?" Jarrod asked.

"You know I'm not," Billy said. "It's just I know Jake—I like him. And Alice has always been—well—just Alice, you know? You say a thing happened, it happened…"

"Keep that in mind," Jarrod said. Then, after a pause, "But you may be right about that Mandy. Caught her giving me the eye just today."

Foreman noticed how the man's voice changed when he asked this. Foreman knew Alice. She was one of the ladies down at the market. She was always friendly, and Foreman knew from listening to his mama talk that Jake, Alice's husband, farmed a small plot just south of town.

Foreman frowned. He didn't know what it meant to be "all over" someone, but he knew it must be bad. Only things that hurt or upset people made Jarrod laugh like that, and only something very wrong would make Billy talk back to his friend. Again, he wished the two of them would just go back to work.

Foreman remained very still, and eventually the two men walked off in separate directions. Foreman returned to his sweeping, hoping it didn't take him long to forget.

Chapter Two

Cletus J. Diggs pulled in to the Quick-Stop and cut the engine. It was going on noon, and he'd already put in a full day. The court over in Hertford had been in session since early morning, and Cletus had pulled double duty, standing for his buddy Jasper as common law attorney on a misdemeanor hunting on private property charge and covering the DUI trial of a local politician for the paper.

A lot of work had gotten done, but Cletus was ready for a twelve-pack of something cheap and cold and WWE Smackdown on the tube. There was only so much a man could be expected to do in one day.

Old Mill was what you'd find in the dictionary if you looked up sleepy little town. The Quick-Stop served as the redneck version of a 7-Eleven. Three stop lights away the road wound on back to Highway 17, past the Hess Station that provided beer and gas to the other end of town.

In between there was a small post office, a pair of antique stores, a hardware store and a garage that was closed as often as it was open. There was nothing earth-shattering going to happen in Old Mill, and that was fine. There were at least five churches, a couple of dozen historical homes, the burned ruin of the old lodge house down by the river, and the park.

The sight of that place always gave Cletus a cold chill. He had been inside while it burned, and only just escaped with mind, body and sanity intact. It reminded him that, no matter how quiet the place might seem, and might actually be—it had a history. America doesn't have many really old places, but Old Mill, North Carolina—tucked up against the depths of The Great Dismal Swamp—was one.

This day Cletus was occupied with other matters, and twelve of them were waiting for him in the cooler at the back of the Quick-Stop.

He climbed out of his truck and stretched. He saw that the sheriff's car was parked in the corner of the lot, and he checked quickly to be sure he didn't have any empties in his truck bed. He knew he should probably glance at his license plate to be sure he'd remembered to pay his registration, but he didn't want to draw attention.

He needn't have worried. Sheriff Bob was inside, leaning on the counter and sipping strong, black coffee—probably stronger and older than was wise. Cletus spotted him through the window and waved. Bob nodded, but made no move away from the counter. Cletus started forward, skirting the edge of the gas pumps and headed for the door.

He didn't make it. Just as he passed the pumps, a loud, sonorous voice rolled around the corner and he stopped. The hesitation was a mistake. He knew that voice, and he knew his only escape lay in making for the door before he was seen.

By the time he got his legs moving, a tall black man in army fatigues and a blue baseball cap rounded the corner and fixed him with a steely glare.

"Yea-yah!" the man cried.

"Hey, Foreman," Cletus said. He kept moving, hoping he might make the door before it was too late. No such luck.

Foreman stepped between Cletus and the door and raised one hand in a peace sign that looked anything but peaceful.

"She wo're MAH WIFE!" the big man said.

"That's cool," Cletus said. He slipped to one side and angled for the door.

"They said ah KILLED her." Foreman insisted, moving closer. His voice was a deep, booming thing that could have put most loudspeaker systems to shame.

Foreman was tall. If he bathed, it wasn't regularly. He always moved too close to whoever he talked to, and it was impossible to know if he understood how uncomfortable it made others. His size, and his unnerving, unwavering stare, had been known to send strangers stumbling and running for cover.

Cletus felt bad for Foreman. As big as the man was, he suffered his share of ridicule from the local kids. Sometimes they followed behind him and threw things, or ran up to try and steal his hat.

No one seemed to know Foreman's whole story. He always wore the fatigues, and as he walked through the town, he stood straight and tall. It gave people the impression he might have been a veteran, but Cletus knew that Foreman had lived near Old Mill all of his life. There was no military service in his past, whatever the explanation for the bearing and the clothing. Walking every day in all forms of weather had worn away any sense of age—Foreman might have been thirty-five, or sixty. He was tall and solid, but difficult to nail down in a description.

In any case, Cletus didn't have the time or inclination to dwell on it.

"See you, Foreman," he said, brushing past the man and pushing through the door of the Quick-Stop with a quick exhaled breath of pure relief. Foreman didn't follow. One glare from Sheriff Bob stopped him in his tracks. As often as not, Foreman got kicked out of any establishment he invaded. He wasn't good for business, and he rarely bought anything more than a cup of coffee.

The door closed behind Cletus, and he leaned against it for a second, getting his mind straight. Bob smiled and raised his coffee.

"Hey, Cletus," he said. "You and your buddy reminiscing out there?"

Cletus frowned. He ignored Bob and headed for the back wall and the beer. The Quick-Stop had an odd assortment. They had cheap, low-end beer, specialty brews with lime and other odd additives, Lite, light, and lighter and some new crap claiming only 64 calories per can.

Cletus grabbed a twelve-pack of Busch. The Quick-Stop was expensive, but the only other option was the Food Lion over in Hertford. Most folks paid the extra money rather than make the drive.

"Planning a party?" Bob asked.

"Party of one," Cletus said. "I got Smackdown on the VCR, and it's been a long day."

Bob nodded, distracted.

"Wonder what that guy's story is?" he said. He nodded out the window to where Foreman still stood, legs in a wide "V," hands folded over his chest. It was like he was standing guard over the town.

Cletus followed Bob's gaze, then shook his head.

"No idea. I could write a book where every chapter was a different story someone told me. Wish he didn't have to stalk me every time I come here."

Bob didn't say anything for a moment.

"Damn shame," he said at last. "Doesn't seem to have a friend in the world. Never sees his family; walks into town every day, alone, and then back home again."

Cletus paid for his beer. He'd never thought much about Foreman's situation. He'd been too caught up in trying to avoid the guy and his booming repetitive story.

"Guess you're right," he said. "Never paid that much attention to him, truth be told. I think he lives out near the edge of town, but now that I think about it, I couldn't tell you exactly where."

"Maple and Old Carolina," Bob said. "I've had to take him there more than once. He lives with an aunt. Skinny woman works down at the nursing home. You don't see her in town much, and if you did, you wouldn't take much notice."

Cletus frowned. It didn't seem like much of a life for a man. He'd already felt bad for not knowing anything about Foreman's past. The last thing he needed was to learn that it was even worse than he'd thought.

"Jesus, Bob," he said. "How do they get by?"

"The way I heard it," Bob said, "she inherited the house and some money. Foreman sweeps sidewalks and does some cleaning. If you ignore his 'show' and insist on it, you can get the man to talk."

"I'll be damned," Cletus said. "Maybe one of these days I'll do that. Could be I could get the whole story out of him. Too tired today."

He took his beer and turned back toward the door. Through the window he saw that Foreman was moving away down the street. He waited until he was sure the man wouldn't turn back, and then said goodbye to Bob and stepped outside.

The sun had started to drop toward the rooftops on River Road. Cletus started across the parking lot toward his truck, and then stopped. Something glinted in the slanting rays of sunlight, and he glanced down to see what it was. On the ground was a black, folded book with a brass clasp. Cletus leaned down and picked it up.

The initials J. P. were etched into the metal. He held it up and frowned. It had looked like any diary when he spotted it—now he saw that it was old. He had the impression it had been carried a lot of miles in someone's pocket.

Cletus glanced around. No one was in sight. He considered going back in and leaving the thing with Bob, or with Louis, the old guy who owned the Quick-Stop. Then he glanced down at it again, and tucked it into his pocket. He could give it a look while he polished off the beer. It was probably just a travel log some trucker used to track his mileage, or a notebook shopping list. Whoever lost it might want it back enough to offer a reward.

Cletus turned out of the parking lot onto the main drag and drove slowly through town. He took a left onto 17. Before long he turned down the narrow, twisting lane that led back to his trailer. As he took the final turn, he slowed to a stop, climbed out, and checked his mail. Beneath the box a long string of wooden placards dangled. Reverend Diggs. Common Law Attorney. Licensed, bonded Auctioneer. There were half a dozen more, reaching almost to the ground.

Cletus had credentials, business cards, IDs and records to back up the claims of every one of those narrow strips of wood. He had more mail order degrees than the swamp had catfish, according to his buddy Jasper.

He just liked playing the odds. He figured the chances of his eating, drinking, and paying the bill for his satellite TV and Internet were better the more business opportunities he was able to tackle. It was also pretty common for him to pick up an investigating job, represent one or the other party legally, preside over the next marriage and/or funeral and write about it for one of the tabloids. Life in Old Mill could be complicated, for all its simplicity.

He sorted through the mail quickly. There were several junk ads, credit card companies spending millions on direct mail programs that Cletus liked to point out as fiscal irresponsibility.

"If they think that's a good outlet for that kind of cash," he'd told his buddy Jasper, "I guess I don't need to ask why they need twenty-seven percent interest."

There were a few bills and a couple of checks from The Weekly Globe. Nothing of particular significance, and that suited him fine. He wasn't looking for a new challenge at that moment.

He climbed back into the truck, drove the few hundred feet to the trailer, parked, and climbed out, the beer dangling from one hand. Without a backward glance at the world, he unlocked the door and disappeared inside.

Cletus' home doubled as an office and research facility. In one corner his old wooden desk sat with the computer on top. Most of the surface of the desk was clear—it was where he worked. The same could not be said for the rest of the place. Every available surface was piled high with folders, books, magazines and clippings.

Cletus didn't entertain much. When he did, they cleared his old couch and gathered in front of the big screen. There was plenty of room to sit, and as Jasper always commented, the way was "clear to the beer."

Cletus put the twelve-pack in his refrigerator. Before he closed the door, he yanked one out and took it, along with the strange old diary, back to his desk. He sat down, popped the top on the beer, took a long swallow and flipped open the shiny metal clasp.

The leather was old and worn, but in surprisingly good condition. It looked as if it might have been rubbed with saddle soap. The pages were yellowed and stiff, but intact. Cletus rubbed a page between his fingers. He thought there was a high linen content in the paper. As old as it was, it must have been fairly expensive when it was new.

The name just inside the front cover stopped Cletus cold.

"Jarrod Pope" was scrawled across the page in bold script. "From your father, on your graduation."

Cletus sat back for a minute. Jarrod Pope was one of the most powerful men in the area. His family had grown cotton since before the Civil War. In more recent years they'd parceled out their land and gotten into the seedier side of real estate. Hardly a week went by that Cletus didn't see one of the Popes down at the courthouse answering charges as slum lords, or seeking an eviction notice and an officer with the balls to serve it down on the poor side of town.

Jarrod was the worst of them. He was in his late fifties,

barrel-chested with a too-red face, jowls that dangled near to his collar. He spoke with a booming, arrogant voice that was seldom silent.

It was nearly impossible for Cletus to imagine the man carrying a personal journal. Hell, it was hard believing the rednecked jerk could write.

Cletus turned the page and started to read. At first all he found was a series of dates, times, and figures. He found an entry where Jarrod had met with his buddy, Billy-Bob, back in the days when Billy-Bob hadn't been too old for the nickname to sound ridiculous.

Then things shifted. There was a last entry that looked like an appointment. It turned out to be a date. There was a woman's name penned carefully next to an address and a time. Mandy Winslow was the name. It meant nothing to Jarrod, but he noted that the script was cleaner at this point, less scribbled and more precise.

"Must've been a hot date," Cletus said, chuckling.

He downed the first beer, got up, and retrieved another from the refrigerator. He tried to imagine himself going to visit Jarrod, returning the book, and telling the man he found it in the Quick-Stop parking lot. Cletus didn't know much about Jarrod Pope's social life, but if that man had set foot in the Quick-Stop in the last decade, Cletus would've eaten his hat. It just made no sense. That meant either someone had stolen the book, which could mean a reward, or that someone else entirely had dropped it.

Cletus took another long sip of beer and flipped through the pages. He came to one that was different from those that had come before it. There was a full entry, like an actual diary page. He read the first lines, frowned, and then his eyes opened very wide.

In the same bold script as the remainder of the book, Cletus read.

"She was my wife. They said I killed her..."

Chapter Three

Cletus pulled into the parking lot at the library and sat, staring at the door. He knew the answers he was after were inside. He also knew Pearl Jackson was inside. He wasn't quite sure what was going to happen when he added himself to the mix.

Pearl Jackson was 250 pounds of attitude with a Dewey Decimal-coded brain. She'd been shelving and dispensing books at the Old Mill Public Library for nearly thirty years. Generations of children had slipped in and out of the stacks of the small library, trying to avoid her prying eyes, or more recently trying to slip past the parental controls on the two Internet-connected computer terminals.

The first time Cletus had poked his head in that door to find a copy of The Adventures of Robin Hood for a book report, Pearl had been there, glaring at him across the desk. She'd made the act of signing up for a library card seem like he was making a pact with the devil. Every time Cletus had entered the library over the years, Pearl had been there, watching and waiting. For what, he was never certain.

It had been almost a year since Cletus had borrowed his last book. It had been a book-on-tape (old-school audio). Fifteen audiocassettes had been enough to get him through about a week of driving around, sitting through stakeouts, and the last fifteen minutes or so before bed.

The book had been a snooze. He'd picked it up because it was new and a best-seller. He'd read nearly every title the small library had to offer. At the time, in stores, and even on the Internet, audiobooks had been pricey, the cheapest running about thirty bucks. He'd learned to buy them and sell them on eBay when he was done, or to trade them in for other titles at the used bookstore in Elizabeth City, but more and more, as time passed and the number of titles available grew too slowly, what they had available was, more often than he liked, just not his cup of tea. He took them anyway. The hours weren't going to pass themselves, and on occasion something he never would have read otherwise ended up catching his attention—and becoming a favorite. Not that last one.

That one had plodded along like a turtle in thick mud. Still, he'd made it through the first ten of the fifteen cassettes and was damned if he'd let it go without at least finding out what in hell happened at the end.

He'd never found out. He'd left the tapes and the portable cassette player he'd bought at the "Everything Less Than Ten Dollars" store on the front seat of his truck one night down at The Cotton Gin. When he'd stumbled out, uncertain he could manage to drive himself home, he'd found the passenger-side window broken out, and the tape player gone. They also, as if to rub it in, had taken the damned book—on-tape.

Cletus knew the boys most likely to have perpetrated the crime and it pissed him off. Not one of them would listen to a book-on-tape, even if it was porn. He figured they'd thought it might be worth something, then tossed it when their parents told them how out-of-date cassettes were, and that you can't pawn or sell a library book.

When Cletus reported the theft to Pearl, she was sympathetic. She was also insistent that theft or not, he owed the library forty-five dollars to replace the book. He explained it to her again. The second time around he even went so far as to claim he'd done the town a favor, since the book had sucked, and now no one would have to be subjected to it.

None of it had fazed her. Less than a week later a bill arrived at Cletus' trailer for forty-five dollars plus tax. He'd called and explained again. More than once, in fact. Each time Pearl had been a little less sympathetic about the break-in and a little more insistent about the bill.

He hadn't called in the last six months. Now he wasn't sure if he should even go inside. He pulled out his wallet with a sigh and counted out two twenties and a five. He stuffed them into the pocket of his flannel shirt, climbed out of the truck and approached the door.

Pearl was nowhere to be seen when he slipped inside, and he breathed a little more easily. The local history, records, and works by notable North Carolinians were tucked into a small alcove, just off the main room of the library. Cletus stepped into that area, scanned the shelves, and found the local history. He walked into that aisle and began studying the titles on the spines, many of which were very old.

There was only one local paper, and it had been published in the same building by the same family since just after the Civil War. There was one each of every issue in the library, fifty-two a year, regular as clockwork. They had been carefully bound, year after year, into leather boards with ribbed spines. There was one blank spot between May of 1920 and the middle of July that same year. A fire had taken down the old library, gutting it completely.

The papers, up until that date, had been off at the bindery being turned into the leather volumes he now stared at, and so had miraculously escaped destruction. Cletus found it ironic that the only time in the history of the library that you could find nothing about was the one time anything important had happened there, but this was a bit of conjecture he kept to himself.

In any case, he was after something more recent. The entries in Jarrod Pope's book were dated and Cletus figured a murder should have been front page news. He also hoped, though he was less optimistic, for something about Foreman.

He guessed Foreman must be closing in on fifty years old, though he carried it well for a crazy man. Jarrod Pope was in his late sixties, getting on in years, as they say, though he still had the energy to bring misery to others in buckets when the mood stuck him.

He'd nearly managed to get the volume for 1942 off of the shelf before a whiff of Chanel No. 5 wafted across the room to him. He knew the floor creaked, so he stood where he was, trying not to breathe.

"You find what you want, Cletus?" Pearl asked. "Haven't seen you around. Thought maybe you'd moved, since I've now sent you twenty-seven correspondences that you have seen fit to ignore."

"Hey Pearl," Cletus said, releasing the spine of the book and turning slowly. "You know, I've been meaning to get in..."

"Save it, Cletus. I know you didn't even open the bills I sent. If you had you'd have seen the last was an announcement of general amnesty. Just bring in your card it said, and we'll wipe the slate clean. I'm guessing you missed that."

"Uh, well," Cletus said, grinning sheepishly, "I have my card here now."

"Amnesty ended two days ago," she said.

Cletus saw the grin spread across her face. He groaned and fished the money out of his pocket.

"Guess I had that coming," he said.

"Guess you did," she agreed.

Pearl took his money, then turned to eye the bound newspapers he'd been about to pull out.

"Those are reference, you know," she said. "They don't leave this room, and you'd best see they get back where they belong. They don't pay me enough to pick up after the likes of you."

"Yes ma'am," Cletus said.

Pearl turned to carry the cash to her desk, but before she'd moved more than a couple of steps, Cletus had another thought.

"Pearl," he called.

She turned and eyed him suspiciously.

"I was wondering," he said. "Back in the day, did you know Jarrod Pope, or Foreman James?"

"Lands sake," she said, staring at him. "Why on earth would you mention those two in the same breath?"

"Just something I'm working on," he said. "I'm looking for a murder that would have happened over forty years ago."

"That old story Foreman hollers about?" Pearl snorted. "I knew his mama. He ain't never had a wife nor even a girlfriend. He's lived here all his life, and what does any of that have to do with Jarrod Pope?"

"I'm not sure," Cletus said. "Maybe nothing. Probably nothing. It's just a hunch. The two of them never worked together, then, I guess?"

Pearl stared at him like he was an idiot. In fact, she looked about to tell him just that when her eyes narrowed and he saw that she'd remembered something.

"How odd," she said. "I would have sworn those two had never come within a mile of one another, but now that you ask, there was a time. When Jarrod was younger, his Papa sent him over to work a spell at the peanut oil factory. Something about learning the value of a dollar."

"Guess he was a good student," Cletus said. "I can't remember a time when he didn't seem to be the richest man around. I'm betting that stint of actual labor didn't sit too well with him. Foreman worked there too?"

"When he was young, before the big fire, yes. He did odd jobs, cleaned up, did pretty much whatever he was told. I remember because I used to think what a fine thing Mr. White had done, giving him the opportunity. Things were hard for the boy's mother as it was. It was strange, too, because there were a lot of folks in need—he didn't see much interested in helping them, but for some reason he took a shine to Foreman."

"What about the father?" Cletus asked. "She was on her own?"

"There were rumors," Pearl said. "There always are. No one was ever quite sure who Foreman's father was. Word had it that it was one of Mr. White's workers. Others said it was a local boy—a white man. These days no one would say boo, but then?"

"I imagine there'd have been quite a stir," Cletus said. "In fact, I'd have expected ol' Jarrod to be one of those who had a problem with it."

"I'm sure he did," Pearl said. "I didn't know him well. Different circles. My mother was a school teacher. Jarrod Pope was sent to boarding school at an early age. His papa said it was the quality of Old Mill's schools, but everyone knew Jarrod was one false step from trouble, even back then. I always figured it was a cover-up of some sort. He didn't come back until he had a college degree, and even then he got sent to the peanut oil factory."

Cletus turned and eyed the bound volumes of the Old Mill Patriot on the shelf. "Don't suppose he was married?" he said.

"Not that I ever heard, at least not until Gracie Wicks caught his eye. He must have been in his thirties by then. Why?"

"I'm not sure yet," Cletus said. "Guess I'd better get busy. If I figure it out, I'll let you know."

"You do that," she said. "And next time you're in, check out the audio section. We've got quite a few new ones in..."

Cletus grinned at her.

"I may do that, but first I reckon I'll need a new alarm system in the truck."

Pearl shook her head and walked back to her desk. Cletus pulled down three volumes of the paper and began to read.

SPECIAL FREE NOVEL PREVIEW

CROCKATIEL - A Novel of the O.C.L.T.

Featuring Cletus J. diggs

About the O. C. L. T. Series

There are incidents and emergencies in the world that defy logical explanation, events that could be defined as supernatural, extraterrestrial, or simply otherworldly. Standard laws do not allow for such instances, nor are most officials or authorities trained to handle them. In recognition of these facts, one organization has been created that can. Assembled by a loose international coalition, their mission is to deal with these situations using diplomacy, guile, force, and strategy as necessary. They shield the rest of the world from their own actions, and clean up the messes left in their wake. They are our protection, our guide, our sword, and our voice, all rolled into one.

They are O.C.L.T.

AVAILABLE & UPCOMING TALES OF THE O. C. L. T.

AVAILABLE NOW:

Brought to Light: An O.C.L.T. Novella by Aaron Rosenberg
The Parting – An O.C.L.T. Novel by David Niall Wilson
The Temple of Camazotz: An O.C.L.T. Novella by David Niall Wilson
Incursions: An O.C.L.T. Novel by Aaron Rosenberg
The Noose Club – an O.C.L.T. Tie-in Novel by David Bischoff
Disciples of the Serpent – an O.C.L.T. Tie-in novel by S. G. Williams

COMING SOON:

Digging Deep – an O.C.L.T. Novel by Aaron Rosenberg

ALSO AVAILABLE

THE ORDER OF THE AIR

An Original Series by Melissa Scott & Jo Graham
Tie-in to the O.C.L.T. in the past

Lost Things
Steel Blues
Silver Bullet
Wind Raker
Oath Bound

Acknowledgments

This book would not have happened without my daughter's and my love of bad SyFy channel movies. It started as nothing more than a title, a game of putting the names of two creatures together into one to see what would make a good movie title. Since our two birds, who have since moved to a bigger home with a lot of other birds, were cockatiels, and we live near the Great Dismal Swamp, Crockatiel was too good to miss. This is – then – a tribute to one heck of a cool bird, Tiki Kowalski, and his buddy Gypsy.

I'd also like to thank Sue Seidel, for agreeing that including Al Seidel as a character in this book was a fitting tribute to an amazing man. Also included are Steve Hislop, Len McMullan, Chuck Gainey, and John Siemens. Crossroad Press fans will note the presence of one "Eddy Dodd" in the prologue of the novel… I bet you can figure out who that is.

I'd also like to thank the love of my life Patricia Lee Macomber for putting up with me laughing and chuckling through the writing of this book. She's tolerated Sharknado and Sharknado 2 – not to mention an endless stream of giant drug-enhanced snakes, ancient artifacts, and unlikely storms on the TV – all contributing to this.

And thank you to North Carolina for providing the setting and the basis for so many memorable characters. Cletus J. Diggs is definitely a native son…

Dedication

This book is dedicated to the memory of Al Seidel, Adventurer, Collector, seeker of truth. The one man I would want with me if I was hunting a dinosaur.

Prologue

2004

The heat surrounded Eddie Dodd like a second skin. It drew the moisture out of him, and the mosquitoes to him with relentless indifference, lending weight to the heavy silence. That silence was what tipped him off, just in time, to pull back into the trees and off the path. The jungle was never silent, and when it was, there was a reason.

Nature has a pecking order. Big eats small, fast eats slow. When the small, large, fast and slow are all quiet, it's a matter of survival. Despite the rifle slung over his back and the 9mm strapped to his hip, Eddie chose that moment to become one with nature… and he waited.

He had only two more days to get through, half-a-dozen samples to collect, and he could hop a jet back home and chill for a few weeks. The others would be returning to camp, and he knew he should do the same, but something held him still. Not many things could quiet a jungle. In fact, he didn't know of any, though he'd seen a prowling tiger silence a much smaller area, to a much smaller degree. He had never heard so little sound. His breath sounded like a fireplace bellows, and his heart pounded like a drum.

The ground beneath him shivered… and grew still. Then it shook, and moments later he heard the crashing, rending sound of trees being pushed aside. Almost simultaneously, birds burst into flight. Animals erupted around him, a wave of baying, barking, howling life. Eddie stood still as stone.

The tree at his back was thick and old. He was completely concealed behind it, and despite the crashing sounds, he thought anything less than a bulldozer was going to have a hard time shaking it, let alone knocking it down. He considered closing his eyes and just waiting until the jungle returned to its normal cacophony, but couldn't quite bring himself to do it. He was frightened, but he was also curious.

On the far side of the tree something was moving hard and fast on the trail, something heavy enough to shake the ground. He caught the scent of the river – rotting vegetation and mud – but he had no time to dwell on this. A scream broke the silence with the force of a rushing train. Eddie clapped his hands to his ears, bent double, and pressed back into the tree so hard he felt as if he might leave an impression in the bark.

He couldn't think. He'd never experienced terror of such magnitude. He'd heard things described as blood-chilling, but had never understood, had never realized, just how real that biting cold could be until it paralyzed him in that forest, thousands of miles from home.

He heard hot, heaving breath. Whatever it was, it was big. Very big. He sensed it pausing on the path, and this time he did hold his breath. He wanted to look. He knew it was the worst thing he could do, the thing that could end him, and yet, he needed to know what was out there, what could make a sound like he'd heard. He stood immobile, fighting his instincts; then the tiger screamed.

It was a primal sound, a warning, and a challenge. There was a second, smaller crashing through the brush, and then an answering roar. Eddie heard a great shifting. Something slammed into the trees to his left, and an answering roar rose. He couldn't stand it.

Keeping very low, hugging the tree tightly, he leaned around the edge.

What met his gaze defied belief. A tiger, claws digging in deep, clung to the long, scaled neck of – what? A dinosaur? It looked something like a crocodile, but so much bigger that any comparison was comical. The neck ended in a long snout and jaws lined with vicious, curved teeth.

"Holy shit," Eddie said.

The tiger was not giving ground. It clung tightly, driving its fangs deep into flesh and digging at the thing's neck and shoulders with its huge back claws. The beast whipped its head back and forth like a trapped serpent, but the big cat had it and was not letting go.

Rearing up, the creature lurched, driving back into the trees, trying to rip the tiger loose. At first it seemed as if it wouldn't work, and then, sensing that it was about to be slammed into a thick trunk, the big cat released and sprang free. It launched from the giant reptile's back with a great driving kick and disappeared into the shadows.

Unable to right itself in time, the creature slammed into the jungle. Its tail whipped around and crashed into the solid trunk of the tree behind which Eddie stood, petrified. It missed him by less than a foot, sending a spray of blood and scales and bark down to shower over him. He let it all come, covering him in bark and leaves and gore, and did not move.

Then the thing was up, shaking its snout in rage and pain. It screamed again, and Eddie couldn't even find the strength to cover his ears. He pressed back into the tree, dripping with blood, dirt and sweat, half afraid he'd wet his pants and not caring.

It turned, then. Without a glance in his direction, it crashed off through the brush, ignoring the path, bending large trees out of its way and clambering over and around others... and it was gone.

Eddie listened, but there was nothing. That – thing – and the tiger, were gone. He still couldn't move. He was having difficulty breathing."What the hell," he said softly, using the sound of his voice to return himself to reality, "was that?"

He crept around the tree and stared at the trail. There were huge gouges in the dirt where the creature's claws had gripped, branches and leaves littered the ground, and all of it was splattered liberally with blood. He stepped into the open and stopped to listen. He heard nothing. The silence did not comfort him. Silence was what had ushered the thing into his reality in the first place.

He made a quick circuit of the cleared space, and found that several large strips of skin had been torn from the injured beast's wounds. It was scaled. He dropped to one knee and looked more closely. It wasn't like anything 'he'd seen before, exactly, but his first impression was still the strongest. It had looked like the biggest damned crocodile in the world. Then, unable to reconcile the images, he shook his head.

He knew what he'd seen. The beast hadn't walked upright, exactly, but it had been able to rise up, to move on only its hind legs.

He tried to focus his memory on the image of it, the shape, the way it had moved, but found his thoughts were muddied. He could only remember snapshots – the tiger, the scream – they were clear.

He glanced down at the slice of skin and made his decision. He wasn't coming back to this jungle again, and he needed a crocodile sample to get out. Damned if he cared if it was some mutant crocodile that ran around on its back feet fighting tigers, he was going home. He knew he couldn't tell anyone what he'd found. No one would believe him, and if they did believe, then they would want to come back – try to find the creature, to hunt it. They would want him along as guide, and, though he'd never considered himself a coward, he knew he'd never be able to do it. The creature's scream still echoed in the back of his mind.

He retrieved his pack and set to work. Moments later, samples secured, he rose and started back down the path. At first, he tried to be stealthy, but every sound, every movement brought back images of the creature, and of the tiger, and before he'd gone twenty yards he'd broken into a trot, and then a flat run. He didn't stop until he'd reached his small boat and pointed it out and away from the bank. He only hoped he could calm himself before he reached camp, turn in his samples, and avoid questions. He doubted if he'd sleep until he was on a plane, and out of Brazil, but it would only be one more day. He had enough samples, as long as the others had been as successful. 'They'd break camp in the morning, and be back in civilization a few hours later.

As he pulled away from the bank, he heard a sound in the distance. He couldn't be certain, but he thought it was an impossibly loud, wailing scream. He gunned the engine and did not look back.

PART ONE

Old Mill, NC – 2004

Chapter One

"There's something weird as hell about this sample, Sammy."

Samuel turned, glaring across the small laboratory in irritation. He was a busy man, and he hated interruptions. His work was important, and he was on a timetable. His funding wasn't going to last forever, and he had no intention of returning to his former position as a lab assistant.

Just short of thirty years, thin and beak-nosed, Samuel Montgomery did not cut an imposing figure. To top it off, he drank so much coffee that he was twitchy. His gaze shifted around the room so quickly at times that people said he reminded them of a squirrel on crack. All of this was heightened when he became annoyed.

"What could possibly," he said slowly, "be weird about a DNA sample from a simple crocodile?" he said. "We have vials of similar cells. I could run a slide projector and display them on the walls like a psychedelic 1960s dance party, and none of them – not one – would be in any way remarkable without the accompanying LSD."

Beatrice dropped her glasses to the end of her nose and glared back at him. She was tall, slender but a little more muscular than she was pretty, with wide shoulders and stringy blonde hair tied off in tight pig-tails. For a horrifying second, despite the imminent danger of contaminating the specimen she was working with, Samuel thought she would pop her gum. She did not.

"You know," she said, "I've seen all of those samples. Before you could set up a slide projector, I could draw the damn things on the wall. I know what crocodile DNA looks like."

Samuel waited.

"This," she said at last, flipping her thumb over to point at the bench to her right, "is weird. It think it's crocodile DNA, but I also think there's something wrong with it. What I'm seeing makes no sense, so, if you could haul your skinny butt over here and look at it, I'd be most appreciative."

Samuel slid off his stool and stepped back carefully from his microscope. His own sample would remain viable for another thirty minutes, and he was nearly finished. He stepped up to his bench, carefully annotated his last actions, then turned and crossed to Beatrice's workstation. As his irritation faded, his curiosity took over. She was an odd duck, keeping strange hours and only working with him because she couldn't handle "steppin' and carryin' for the man," in a bigger lab, but she was sharp. Weird was a word she used indiscriminately, though, and could mean anything from a small contamination to a completely new species without enough inflection in her voice to provide a warning.

She slid aside, and Samuel bent to the microscope. He adjusted the focus and stared. Then, very slowly and carefully, he adjusted it again. He didn't move for a long moment, and when he did, it was very slowly.

"What the hell," he said, "is that?"

"You tell me, Einstein. It came in that last cooler from South America. It's marked 'crocodile,' and, as I'm sure you noticed, it's sort of like a crocodile, but..."

"But it's not," he finished. "Damn. I know I've seen something similar to that, but I can't for the life of me remember where. It's like, a mutation, or ..."

"Don't go all Jurassic Park on me, Sammy." Beatrice said, grinning.

Samuel glanced at her and caught the expression. He noted, not for the first time, that it transformed her normally cynical, scowling features into something much more intriguing.

"Don't call me Sammy. Sammy sounds like some down-and-out beatnik or a kid with a paper route."

Beatrice didn't reply. She also didn't look apologetic.

"So?" she prodded.

Samuel pressed his eye back to the microscope and tried to clear his thoughts. He didn't have a photographic memory, but he was close to it. What he had was more like a mental filing cabinet. He could access things given peace – and a little time. This was harder, because he knew Beatrice was watching, and he loved it when he managed to surprise her. Most of the time, he knew, he was a crabby, boring-as-hell academic.

Also, there was this sample. Something about it itched at his memory like a stuck record. He had seen something like it before…

Then he stood, pushed back from the bench, and shook his head.

"What?" she asked. When he didn't immediately answer she repeated it, smacking him on the shoulder. "What?"

"I think…" he hesitated, and then blurted it out, "I'm afraid I can't do as you ask," he said. "I'm afraid I am going to have to go 'Jurassic' on you…or at least, 'Cretaceous'. I have seen this before. It's a crocodile all right, a very old one. I knew it was familiar, but now I remember from where. It was a simulation of Sarcosuchus DNA."

"Sarco what?" Beatrice asked, frowning. "What the hell are you babbling about?"

"Dinosaurs," he said. "Sarcosuchus was an ancestor of the modern croc… sort of like a smaller version of a T-Rex with a long snout, built low to the ground."

Beatrice stared at him.

"So," she said slowly, "you saw a simulation of something very old, and now, after a couple of moments of contemplation, you've decided that the DNA sample under my microscope is, what, a few million years old?"

"No, of course not," Samuel said, distracted. "At least 100 million, probably a bit more. Early Cretaceous Period, if memory serves… it pretty much always does."

"And so," Beatrice continued, "somewhere down in Brazil, there's a dinosaur running around loose? That's what you think?"

"It has nothing at all to do with what I think, does it?" he snapped. "It's not like I slipped it to you, or made it in my basement. It's right there on the slide, and I'm telling you, I know what it is. Remains of Sarcosuchus have been found in Africa, and in parts of South America."

"Let me guess," Beatrice sighed. "Brazil?"

Samuel nodded.

They both stared at the microscope as if it might hop off the bench and chase them around the room.

"Well, hell," Beatrice said at last. "I guess we won't be using that sample."

Samuel turned and stared at her. Then, very slowly, his irritation drained away and he actually smiled. Then, softly at first, growing rapidly in strength, Samuel Montgomery began to laugh. Unable to stop herself, Beatrice joined him. It was a long time before they regained enough control to store the sample and separate the rest of the batch it had come from.

"So who do we tell?" Beatrice asked, as they sealed the refrigerator. "I mean, holy crap, who finds dinosaur cells? Where did they come from? Is there one of these things out there still alive, or is this just some odd genetic throwback – some big king croc that had cells he should not be carrying embedded in his code?"

"All good questions," Samuel said. "The answer to the first, and most important, is no one. If we hand this over to anyone – if we even let it slip that we might have come in contact with it – it will disappear so quickly we'll hardly remember it existed. This is our ticket. We have to guard it, study it – and most importantly, we have to prove it is what I say it is."

"How?" Beatrice asked.

When she saw his grin, she shook her head. "No," she said. "No way. I've seen the movies. You can't be serious…"

"Oh, I am," Samuel said. "Not a fully formed creature, but the cells…they are still fresh. We can grow cultures, study them and learn. We'll have all we need to write the paper that will put us on the map. No more sexing pet birds or tracing the lineage of the local Pekingese."

"Jesus," Beatrice said. "You're serious."

"I am," he said, and nodded. "Very."

"I'm not doing this now," she said. "Not today. I think I need a drink. A very strong drink."

"If you don't mind," Samuel said, still smiling, "I believe I will join you. Tomorrow will be soon enough. We're going to have to knock off the regular work rather quickly to make the time…"

"Enough," she said. "No more. Drinks. Sleep."

Samuel nodded absently, lost in thought.

"I think," he said, "I'm going to be having bourbon. Lots of it."

"I'll see that and make it double," Beatrice said. "Let's lock up and get the hell out of here."

Chapter Two

"Will you please do something about those damned birds? My god, do they ever shut up?"

Neal smiled, but was careful to conceal the expression behind a cough. Katrina was pissed, and he didn't want to fuel the fire. In the next room, Tiki and Gypsy, their Cockatiels, were screeching and wolf whistling, making sounds like ray guns and cartoon spaceships, and had been doing so for about twenty minutes straight. It was nothing new, but sometimes the pair got out of control, and they were loud. He thanked the gods a last time they hadn't decided on a cockatoo. Those birds could be heard for up to two miles.

"I'll take care of them," he said. He rose and grabbed his guitar, heading into the other room. When he got inside, he closed the door behind him, then opened the cage. The two birds chirped a last couple of times, but all they had wanted was a chance to get out and stretch their wings. Neal bent down, took each on one of his fingers, and transferred them to his shoulders.

Then he sat down at his desk and drew the guitar into his lap. He liked to combine time with the birds and his music. It was a hobby – at one time it might have been more, but he'd chosen other trails. Now he played and sang because he enjoyed it, not really caring what anyone thought.

Gypsy, the more curious of the birds, hopped carefully down his arm and shuffled toward the neck of the guitar.

"No you don't," he said. He took her on his finger again and moved her to the desk, where she began contentedly shredding the top page of the manuscript he'd been editing. It didn't matter. He had it all on the computer. He left the paper out for the dual purposes of keeping the bird busy and providing a shield against droppings. Anyone who has spent any time with birds knows, shit happens. A lot.

Tiki Kowalski, the bigger, bolder bird stayed put. He was happy to perch on Neal's shoulder, and would stay there until he either got bored and took flight to the top of his cage for a snack, or was put away. The only thing he liked better than sitting on Neal's shoulder was courting Gypsy… which was the problem.

Tiki had a very distinctive mating song. The votes were not in yet on whether Gypsy was even a female. They'd searched websites and found inconsistent "rules" for sexing birds, but nothing conclusive. They'd even taken a feather that came loose when Gypsy took a wild flight around the house, escaping her room and panicking in the larger space beyond. She'd hit a wall, and Neal had caught her, like a basket catch by Willie Mays. The feather, collateral damage, he'd snagged and bagged. He already had a similar feather from Tiki, just in case his mating virtuosity was that of a female seeking a mate.

The one sure way to sex a pet bird is to send off a DNA sample for analysis. Not horribly expensive, but you needed a sample – a blood feather was perfect. He'd been hoping to prove that Gypsy was a girl, and Tiki was absolutely a male. They didn't want baby birds, but there seemed no real danger of that. Gypsy, while not exactly rejecting Tiki's advances, was certainly never in an amorous mood. Tiki was not fazed – he had developed a song and a dance. The family called it the Tiki Tango, and once he got going, he was a force of nature. Almost nothing could stop him until the song had run its course. Gypsy had learned to mimic the song, but it wasn't quite the same. Neal had even made the irritating ditty his ring tone for a while, resulting in some odd looks at business meetings.

He turned his attention to the guitar. He'd been trying to perfect a favorite song by Passenger, he thought it was titled "'Let her go," but wasn't sure. For some reason the lyrics of the simple chorus kept jumbling in his head. It didn't help that Tiki started almost immediately picking at the chain that held the lucky penny around his neck, pulling and digging in with his not insubstantial claws.

After a few runs through the song, Neal set the guitar aside and took Tiki on his finger.

"Asshole," he said. "I was about to get it."

Tiki tilted his head to one side and reached out, gripping Neal's glasses and tugging playfully. Gypsy, meanwhile, had grown bored with the paper, and the desk, and hopped to Neal's arm. When Tiki noticed, he sidled slowly over, and Neal couldn't help laughing.

"No you don't, pal," he said. "Mommy is already pissed off at you and your big mouth. No Tiki Tango for you today. I'll get you two some millet and you can get back in that cage. I'm closing the door, and you are going to shut up, if you know what's good for you."

He carried them back to their cage, filled their food dishes with seeds and pulled their millet holder out. They loved the stuff. Kat called it "crack" for Cockatiels. It came in long, branch-like "sprays" that he tucked into a plastic tube and hung from the disco-ball toy in the center of their cage. He knew it would be decimated by the next day, but it would also, mostly, keep them quiet.

He grabbed his guitar and left the room, closing the door behind him to block the sound in case the millet failed in its mission. Kat really loved the birds, but when they got noisy, they could try the patience of a saint.

He carefully tucked the Martin back into its case, smiling as he did so. He'd worked a lifetime to own an instrument like this. He probably should still have waited, but Kat had insisted he go ahead and get it. It was one of those special things that could always make him smile. The birds were like that too, and the dogs, and the cats, and all the other animals that had made their way through the zoo they called a house.

Most of their kids had moved on to lives of their own. Their youngest, Mary, was ten, and loved the animals like they did. All their lives they had lived with the certain knowledge that there had to be a secret symbol on the outside of their house that said "Suckers live here" in cat, dog, and several other animal languages. Nothing else could explain the menagerie.

He closed the guitar case and headed to the kitchen for a drink. Kat was checking on the crockpot full of chili, and Neal's mouth watered as he came up behind her, wrapping her in a hug. He'd also waited a lifetime for the chance to spend the rest of that same life with someone who cared – someone who actually loved him, probably more than he deserved. She also made a mean pot of chili.

"I'm going to move them out into the garage," she said.

He knew she didn't mean it, but he wished that the animals would listen. Not for the first time, he thought the perfect super power would be the ability to communicate with them. Flying would be cool, super strength would come in useful, but how much could you learn and know if you understood what the birds and wolves, bears and bulls, and goddam Cockatiels, for that matter, were thinking and saying? At least he might convince Tiki not to crap on Kat's shoulder...

"They're settled down," he said. "I think Tiki is getting a little amorous... must be in the air." He kissed her on the neck.

She turned and raised an eyebrow. "As far as we know, Tiki and Gypsy are both boys, and all he's going to get is pecked on the head."

"We'll know soon," Neal said.

Kat shook her head.

"I can't believe you sent them a feather. Really? All the things you could worry over, and you choose sexing a Cockatiel."

"You're just afraid Gypsy will be a girl. Then you'll know when Tiki sits on your shoulder and 'chirps the bird,' he's serious."

"You're a jerk."

"But you love me."

She leaned back into him and laughed. In the other room, Tiki started singing again, and Neal laughed too.

"Is it working for you?" he asked.

She turned and whacked him on the arm.

"I hate the bird," she said. She was still laughing.

"I know," he said. "I know. He hates you too, but it's a love/hate thing."

Without warning, he scooped her up in his arms and carried her to the bedroom. Before they got inside, he lifted his head and started whistling, mocking Tiki's song.

"You want to survive," she said, kissing him, "you'll quit while you're behind."

He laughed again and kicked the door closed behind them. They had about an hour before their daughter would return home, and he didn't want to waste it. There were far too few times when they were alone. Faintly, he could still hear Tiki singing, but he held the laugh. No sense spoiling a perfect moment.

Chapter Three

Samuel sat in the lab, staring at a set of cultures, a tray of test tubes and the clock. He had been working steadily for fourteen hours. Beatrice had gone out for sushi and left him to finish up, but he couldn't bring himself to finalize the day's work. It was so important, so momentous, that the thought of closing it down and moving into a seemingly endless period of waiting maddened him.

As it turned out, they'd had enough of the sample to set up three separate cultures. They had agreed to try with the first and preserve the others so that, on the chance they succeeded and something amazing actually happened – a thing they both believed likely but could not bring themselves to count on – they would have proof to back up their work and something for the inevitable follow-on doubters to use in recreating their results. The important thing was that they were first to the table, well-documented, and credited for the work.

Samuel had spent a long life being so detail conscious he'd been called anal on more than one occasion and actually examined during his childhood to be certain his desire to color code his socks and arrange his toys by size, shape, and the year he'd received them on his shelves was not severe OCD. He just didn't believe in disorganization. It was a trait that had served him well in this small lab, and less well in larger corporations where he didn't have the authority to arrange things the way he liked them. He realized it was a strength as well as a problem, but it wasn't something he could control, and his efforts to cover for himself always seemed to come off as arrogance.

Here, he was free to keep things any way he liked them. Beatrice didn't share his need for organization, but she appreciated it, and she stayed out of his way. He realized it made her life easier, and he often took this out on her by being grumpy, but they were a good team, and this – this pile of glass and cells and chemicals on the bench in front of him – was their ticket.

Genetics was a field where you could still make a name for yourself. Regardless of what people were led to believe, things like cloning, organ growth, genetic body modification, were not as illegal as the government let on. In fact, there were dozens of think tanks, laboratories, and long-term experiments going on behind the scenes at any given moment – some of them so far out there that even Samuel had a hard time wrapping his head around them.

The thing was that those big programs were littered with genius and ego. One, maybe two people would be remembered on the scene of any true breakthrough, and a lot of the programs the government backed were likely to achieve results one might not want their name associated with, once they finally went public.

This was different. This was the Holy Grail. While science had a good-sized public-interest factor, and some scientists could actually be considered pop icons – it was a serious crapshoot finding something the public cared about long-term enough to sustain viability. If he and Beatrice managed to go Jurassic Park on the world, actually brought a viable dinosaur to life and presented it to the scientific community, that was the key to an amazing future. Movies would be made. Bad SyFy movies would abound.

He glanced at the materials he was working with, picked up the card for the subject identification and laughed. Dinosaurs and birds were so closely related that at times they could be considered evolutionary pairs. Knowing this, and having limited resources, they had shuffled through the samples they had available, and they'd come across a pair of blood feathers, sent in by their owners for sexing. Birds were notoriously hard to pin down without DNA or the actual appearance of fertilized eggs – they represented a large part of the lab's daytime business – and these feathers had both come from a single household, a pair of Cockatiels.

Beatrice had objected at first. Sarcosuchus was a crocodile. A damn big one, but still, a creature that had basically changed very little over the centuries. On the surface, the connection to birds that was all the rage with T-Rexes and other dinosaurs didn't seem to apply. The reality, however, is that crocodiles and birds are more closely associated than most other reptilian creatures could claim, so the DNA link was not as far-fetched as it seemed.

The birds, Tiki Kowalski and Gypsy, bore similar markings. The note that had accompanied the feathers explained that Tiki was aggressive sexually, and it was unclear how Gypsy was reacting. Samuel had seen similar notes a thousand times. Birds were intriguing creatures – he had a very chatty Conure named Livingston that had been his companion for nearly a decade. He'd thought of getting the bird a partner, but, and he was aware how sad the notion was, he was worried that if he did he'd lose time with one of his only friends.

They had sexed the birds, and mailed off the results. Tiki was definitely a male. The slightly less cheerful news was that Gypsy was also a male. The two were friends, but apparently Mr. Tiki Kowalski was one frustrated bird. He hoped the owners would find a way to deal with it, but all he cared about at the moment was that Tiki's cells – culled from the feather – had blended nicely with those of the sample that had come in from Brazil. He wasn't certain what they would end up with when all was said and done, but they'd both agreed that trying for a male – whatever – was safer than having a female that might escape and find a way to mate. After the lesson of Spielberg's films, frog DNA was out of the question. No Cockatiel in either of their memories had suddenly changed sex, as amphibians had been known to. Silly to base fears on fiction, but too much of the science they took for granted had its roots in stories and novels. Besides, what they had done had worked.

They might have been able to clone from just the sample, but it was foreign to anything they were familiar with, and the bonding of the DNA made the work simpler. They could also have used cells from a regular crocodile, but were afraid the result might prove less than exciting. What if it was just a mutation, and when bonded to DNA from a normal creature, just normalized itself and they ended up with an unremarkable crocodile and a lot of wasted time?

So Cockatiels it was. The irony wasn't lost on him. What they were making – what they would bring to life – the breeders who created Schnoodles and Puggles would probably call a damned "Crockatiel" – and he found that he didn't care. As long as it made him famous – as long as he and Beatrice got the credit and something came of it.

"Crockatiel it is," he said softly. "Rise! Live!" He laughed softly.

Then he noticed the sudden pounding of rain, and vaguely, as if the sound was fading in from a distance, he became aware of wind roaring outside. He hadn't known it was going to storm. It would suck driving the crooked road back to town, and he wondered where in hell Beatrice had gotten to.

Outside the lab, the wind had kicked up to nearly fifty miles per hour. The tops of the trees lining the road leading in from the highway had begun to sway, dipping even lower at the press of stronger gusts. The rain, which had started at about the strength of a heavy shower, pounded onto the windshield of Beatrice's Jeep. She fought to keep it on the road, and cursed under her breath.

It wasn't the first time that she and Samuel had managed to overlook things going on in the world around them. They lived insular lives, and they were both focused on their work. Currently that work was fascinating beyond anything she'd ever been involved in, and she'd done little but sleep, rise, eat, work, eat and repeat since they started. She doubted Samuel had taken a single full night to sleep, and was absolutely certain he'd not wasted any time on the news.

Still, managing not to notice the hourly warnings of an oncoming hurricane for nearly two days was a new high – or low – even for them. She'd gotten their food as the restaurant was closing. Early. When she'd asked why, the girl had looked at her like she was crazy and explained about the storm.

"Hurricane Callie is hovering off the North Carolina coast," the radio crackled. "Current radar tracking projects it will cut inland across the Outer Banks and skirt the coast past Hampton Roads before moving north. Callie is a Category Two storm, but projected to grow in strength before landfall. Evacuations are in effect for…"

There was no evacuation in effect where the lab was located, but it was directly in the path of the storm. There was just time for her to get out there, get Samuel, and get out. Despite the danger, Beatrice was thinking of the samples, and the cultures they were processing. She hoped she could convince Samuel to go, but common sense and genius aren't particularly dependent on one another, and she knew it would be a struggle.

She was frightened. She'd been through storms in her hometown, back in Illinois, huge dark thunderstorms and tornadoes that ripped through towns and obliterated everything in their path. It wasn't the same, but she'd spent enough time obsessively viewing footage of hurricanes since moving to North Carolina to have developed a respect bordering on paranoia about them. It didn't help that every time the wind blew hard enough to move a leaf, the local weather men began predicting doom and destruction, or that you could pick up your hurricane survival checklist at any grocery or convenience store.

Beatrice wasn't scared of much. The local rednecks had tried pushing her, courting her, and come up wanting (and hurting, in several instances). Insults to her lifestyle, dress code (or lack thereof) and lack of a social life flowed over her like water. She had long since come to the conclusion that surrounding herself with the things she enjoyed was the only sensible way to live, and that if life sent someone along that happened to be comfortable there – that was great. If not, at least no time would be wasted chasing things she didn't care about, or living up to the expectations of a world that, for the most part, didn't interest her.

This was different. The windshield wipers were having trouble parting the pouring rain long enough to give her a clear view of the road. By the time the lab came into sight, she was almost on top of it. She slowed, wheeled into the parking lot, and pulled to a stop as close to the front door as possible. She glanced at her umbrella, and then realized how quickly it would be destroyed. Instead, she wrapped herself around the box of sushi, leapt out of the Jeep, slammed the door behind her and ran in crazy, splashing strides. Thankfully, Samuel must have been watching for her; he opened the door as she hit the small concrete porch, and she nearly dove inside. He closed the door quickly and stood, blinking and staring.

"What?" she said.

"Nothing," Samuel said. He failed to hide his grin. "You're... wet."

She stared at him. She would have laughed, but her teeth were chattering suddenly, and the wind whipping against the walls and through the trees had begun to sound like the roar of a large train.

"It's a hurricane," she said. "Hurricane Callie. We didn't know... we have to go..."

"Too late, I'm afraid," he said, almost cheerfully.

She stared at him, trying to figure out whether he was stupid, or just hadn't heard her correctly.

"We have to go!" she said.

He grabbed her by the shoulders and steadied her.

"We can't get out of here now," he said. "The winds are too strong. The storm will be here in less than half an hour, and the outer edges are already here. There is nowhere we could drive to that is safer than here, and there is no way we'd make it if we tried. The road will probably flood, but we're on higher ground. We're in this for the long haul, so I need you to calm down and listen."

"But..."

"No buts. I've lived here all my life. I've survived a few of these storms in my time, and I know what I'm doing. Do you know why I chose this building for the lab?"

Beatrice, feeling shell-shocked, bit her lip and shook her head.

"It was built by the Jamieson-Wicks Corporation. They are based right here in North Carolina. Andrea Wicks, the founder? She's probably the world's foremost expert on hurricanes. They say she nearly stopped one once, but that's not important. What is important is that this building is one of her prototypes. It was designed to withstand winds of up to two hundred miles an hour. It has a small generator that runs on propane for up to a week, and I had the tanks filled a while back. The best part? Everyone thought she was crazy. No one bought the buildings, no one bought the technology – at least not below the large, corporate level - and even though I'm pretty sure she and her Navy pilot husband had something to do with Hurricane Andrea, a few years back, only being a little over a Category One when it hit, you don't see people out there trying to stop this one."

"So, you're trusting a crazy woman?" Beatrice asked.

"I trust you, but that's not the point. The point is, in all of this area, there are only a dozen or so buildings as safe as this one during a hurricane, and she built all of them. I got it for a song. The previous owners didn't see the design as a selling point, but I know what I know. We'll be fine."

"What about food?"

Samuel eyed the bag she carried.

"We seem to be covered for this evening," he said. "If we have to stay, we'll be fine. I'm not really much of a survivalist, but this place inspired me. I couldn't help stocking the emergency locker. We have lights, batteries, a radio and a small television set, in case we lose the Internet. We have canned goods, and even some old C-rations I picked up at the Army Navy store up in Virginia."

Beatrice dropped her fists to her hips and frowned at him.

"Where has all of this been?" she asked.

"What do you mean?"

"This!" she said, waving toward the back of the building. "This... normal person preparedness crap. I've known you what, three years now? Not once have you shown the slightest interest in anything but the lab, the work, an occasional beer. Now I find out you're a closet hurricane freak of some kind, you actually prepare for things that don't involve microscopes, and the thought of hundred-mile-an-hour winds doesn't even faze you. Who the hell are you?"

Samuel laughed.

"I told you, I've lived here all my life. Some of that time occurred prior to college, you know. I've always been fascinated by storms. I've seen what they can do, and I respect it. That's why I wanted this building. Andrea Jamieson-Wicks is a personal hero of mine. Can't I have secrets?"

Just then the wind picked up, and the lights wavered, then steadied. Beatrice turned and stared at the window, as if she expected it to implode at any moment.

"While we're questioning things," Samuel said, "what happened to the not-scared-of-anything bitch-chick I hired? It's just some wind and rain…"

"It's wind and rain that could flood the roads, knock down trees, and drown a city," she said simply. "I don't like thunder – I don't like rain. I know, most 'spooky' chicks who wear black and scowl a lot are into dark and stormy nights…not this one. I wish I was a million miles from here…"

"We'll be fine," Samuel repeated. "While we've got Internet, let me show you some things…might not make you feel better, but it might, and it will certainly pass the time better than watching that window…"

About the Author

DAVID NIALL WILSON has been writing and publishing horror, dark fantasy, and science fiction since the mid-eighties. An ordained minister, once President of the Horror Writers Association and multiple recipient of the Bram Stoker Award, his novels include Maelstrom, The Mote in Andrea's Eye, Deep Blue, the Grails Covenant Trilogy, Star Trek Voyager: Chrysalis, Except You Go Through Shadow, This is My Blood, Ancient Eyes, On the Third Day, The Orffyreus Wheel, The DeChance Chronicles, including Heart of a Dragon, Vintage Soul, My Soul to Keep, Kali's Tale and the soon to be released Nevermore, The Parting and The Temple of Camazotz, both for the original series O.C.L.T. and the memoir / cookbook American Pies: Baking with Dave the Pie Guy. David can be found at http://www.davidniallwilson.com and can be reached by e-mail at david@macabreink.com.

David is CEO and founder of Crossroad Press, a cutting edge digital publishing company specializing in electronic novels, collections, and non-fiction, as well as unabridged audiobooks and print titles. Visit Crossroad Press at http://store.crossroadpress.com

Curious about other Crossroad Press books?
Stop by our site:
http://store.crossroadpress.com
We offer quality writing
in digital, audio, and print formats.

Enter the code FIRSTBOOK
to get 20% off your first order from our store!
Stop by today!

Made in the USA
Monee, IL
12 November 2022